M000191298

CAEL

HEROES AT HEART SERIES

MARYANN JORDAN

Cael (Heroes at Heart) Copyright 2018

All rights reserved. No part of this book may be reproduced or transmitted in any form or by any means, electronic or mechanical, including photocopying, recording, or by any information storage and retrieval system without the written permission of the author, except where permitted by law.

If you are reading this book and did not purchase it, then you are reading an illegal pirated copy. If you would be concerned about working for no pay, then please respect the author's work! Make sure that you are only reading a copy that has been officially released by the author.

This book is a work of fiction. Names, characters, places, and incidents either are products of the author's imagination or are used fictitiously. Any resemblance to actual persons, living or dead, events, or locales is entirely coincidental.

ISBN ebook: 978-1-947214-14-9

ISBN print: 978-1-947214-15-6

❀ Created with Vellum

AUTHOR INFORMATION

USA TODAY BESTSELLING AND AWARD WINNING AUTHOR

I am an avid reader of romance novels, often joking that I cut my teeth on the historical romances. I have been reading and reviewing for years. In 2013, I finally gave into the characters in my head, screaming for their story to be told. From these musings, my first novel, Emma's Home, The Fairfield Series was born.

I was a high school counselor having worked in education for thirty years. I live in Virginia, having also lived in four states and two foreign countries. I have been married to a wonderfully patient man for thirty-seven years. When writing, my dog or one of my four cats can generally be found in the same room if not on my lap.

Please take the time to leave a review of this book.

Feel free to contact me, especially if you enjoyed my book. I love to hear from readers!

Facebook

Email

Website

As an adolescent counselor for over twenty-five years, I had the opportunity to work with many young people. One young man, upset over a poor choice he had made, came to me. As I listened to his story and his confession, I told him that the true measure of a man was not in the mistakes he made, but in how he handled those mistakes. I remember the look on his face when I told him I was sure he was going to be a good man.

So, this book is dedicated to all the students over the years who allowed me to be a part of their lives.

Cael Holland was buckled in the back seat of the lady's car, staring out the window. Clutching his small Teddy bear, he felt sick to his stomach and wondered, if he threw up, would she still take him to their destination? Before he had a chance to ponder any further, the car turned down a residential street, houses standing guard on either side of the sidewalks.

The yards were trimmed, some with flowerbeds lining front walks. Others had big bushes near their porches. Massive trees were in every yard, some with swings hanging from their lower branches. Curious, he pressed his nose against the window. The car slowed as it approached the house at the end, and his heart began to pound even harder. Swallowing back the tears that threatened to slide over his cheeks, he thought of his sister and their goodbye.

"Why can't I live with you?" he had cried, clinging to her legs. She was eight years older than he was and in his mind, she was old enough to take care of him.

"Oh, Cael," Kathy said. "I'm just not old enough. I wish I was."

"How old do you have to be to keep me?" he whined.

"I'd have to be a grownup. That won't be for another two years and then I still won't be able to take care of you like you should be taken care of. I'm so sorry."

"Then why can't I stay here with you and Granny?"

A grimace crossed her face, as she admitted, "Granny's old and says she can only keep me since I'm almost grown anyway and can get a summer job to help out. She says she don't got no energy to raise a boy."

Crying harder, he had clung tightly as she wrapped her arms around him.

"Cael, don't cry," she had begged. "Granny says we can stay in touch."

"What if where they take me they don't let me come see you?"

"Then I'll get Granny to bring me to you." Wiping his tears, she held his hand as the social worker approached. Her eyes had been kind but her mannerism hurried. Putting her arm around his shoulders, she guided him to the car and into the back seat, in one fell swoop taking him away from his sister, the only person he had left in the world.

Now, she pulled the car to a stop outside the house at the end of the street. Getting out, she opened his door, motioning for him to follow. "Come along, Cael. Let's go meet your new family." Bending low, she smiled as she said, "You're very lucky. Miss Ethel is the best foster mom we have. You'll like it here."

He knew she was lying to him to get his cooperation, but he pinched his lips together, saying nothing. Climbing out of the seat, he clutched his bear to his chest as she grabbed his suitcase. Following her up the front walk, he spied an older woman coming onto the porch. Tall and thin, she wore a yellow dress with a little black belt, shoes like his granny wore, wire-rim glasses perched on her nose, and her grey hair pulled back in a bun. His feet stumbled and he tripped on the first step, staring up at her.

She smiled, bending low to greet him. "Cael, I'm so glad to have you come to my home. I'm Miss Ethel."

Her smile made his stomach hurt a little less but, as he looked behind her, he spied four little faces plastered against the screen door, all staring at him. His stomach knotted again and he wondered if now was when he would finally throw up.

Miss Ethel glanced behind her and shooed the other boys away. Turning back to him, she smiled once more, saying, "My other boys are so excited to meet you. Let me talk to Ms. Traynor for a moment and then we'll go inside." Patting his shoulder, she stood and took the suitcase from the social worker.

He looked up at the two women conversing, before sliding his gaze back to the door. He could no longer see the other faces, but he heard the slight sounds of whispering coming from inside the house.

"Come along, Cael," Miss Ethel said. "Let's go in. I've got some chocolate chip cookies, fresh out of the oven."

As she opened the screen, the delightful scent of

homemade cookies wafted by and his stomach growled. Turning, he watched the social worker walk back to her car. Without a way to escape, he took a deep breath and followed Miss Ethel into the house, curiosity taking over fear.

With her hand on his shoulder, she stepped into the living room, where he could now clearly see the other boys.

"Boys this is Cael. He's eight years old and I want you to make sure to welcome him as you wanted to be welcomed when you first came to me. Cael, this is the oldest, Zander. He's ten years old."

Cael watched as a tall, dark blond boy with piercing blue eyes stepped forward. His face, hard at first, broke into a grin. "That your bear?"

Holding it tighter, in case Zander chose to take it, he just nodded.

"Cool," Zander said, his smile still in place.

Another boy, dark haired, walked up next. "I'm Rafe," he said. "I'm eight too."

Before he had time to process that there was another boy his age, two younger boys bounded up, both so close in appearance, he had to blink to tell them apart.

"I'm Jayden. This is Jaxon."

"Boys," Miss Ethel said, drawing out the word while lifting her eyebrow. "Behave."

Cael looked up at her in confusion, not under-standing what they had done that she needed to correct.

The two boys broke into giggles, before the one who spoke, said, "Sorry, Miss Ethel." Looking back at him, he said, "I'm actually Jaxon and this is my twin, Jayden."

Their snaggle-toothed grins beamed as they asked Miss Ethel if it was time for cookies.

Laughing, she said, "Bring Cael with you."

Grabbing him by the arm, Zander led them into the dining room. The big table had lots of chairs around it and he climbed into the one next to Zander. The other boys quickly scrambled into their seats and eagerly awaited Miss Ethel's return to the room, her hands full with a tray with glasses of milk and a platter of still-warm cookies.

Looking at the others, not wanting to be left out, he grabbed two cookies to put on his napkin, licking the melted chocolate from his fingers. It had been a long time since he had had cookies this good. His mom used to make them, but that was before. Before his dad died and his mom became so sad she stopped taking care of them. Shoving one delectable treat into his mouth, the warm flavors tickled his tongue and his stomach stopped hurting.

Miss Ethel smiled around the table and made sure the milk glasses were refilled if needed. Licking his lips, he stared in unabashed interest at the other boys. They were all laughing and joking with each other.

Jaxon looked over and cocked his head to the side. "Your hair's kind of funny."

Before he had a chance to react, Miss Ethel's voice rang out. "Jaxon." He watched as the boys immediately quieted and he figured that, when she spoke, they listened.

"I'm sorry. I don't mean nothing bad. It's just a different color."

He had heard his sister talk about his hair being strawberry-blond but never really knew what that meant. Her hair was yellowish and his was kind of orangey-blond, like their dads' had been. "I got my daddy's hair," he said, his words proud, but his stomach clenching again.

"I like it," Jaxon pronounced, an easy grin in place, going back to his cookie.

By the time they were ready for bed, he had finally relaxed somewhat…at least his stomach felt better with dinner and some games afterwards. When they walked upstairs, Miss Ethel took him to the side and spoke to him quietly.

"Cael, in my house, the boys share rooms because that way you all get to know each other real good, like brothers. But, I know this is a big change and can be very scary."

He looked up at her kind face and asked, "Will I ever be able to see my sister again?"

"Oh, sweet boy," she exclaimed, kneeling in front of him. "Yes, of course. She may visit here anytime and I will work with your grandmother to make sure you can visit her there as well."

His shoulders visibly relaxed and he offered her a tremulous smile.

"Cael, remember that nothing's as important as family. Of course, family is not just those we are born into, but the families that we make as well. Your sister is your family, but then so will we become family too. We have room in our hearts to love lots of people."

She cocked her head to the side, peering at him. "Cael. That's an unusual name. Did your parents ever tell you the meaning of your name?"

Shaking his head, he peered up at her in interest.

"The name has a connection to Irish mythology, but is also the name of the archangel associated with the astrological sign of Cancer. From this perspective, Cael is an angel of domestic bliss and nurturing love."

He scrunched his nose in confusion, not understanding her words.

Laughing, she patted his shoulder. "All that means is that you're a very sweet boy who likes to take care of those around him. We're lucky to have you with us."

With that, she stood, pointing out the three bedrooms, giving him a chance to look inside. "Jaxon and Jayden share this room, but there is an extra bed here also." Opening up the other door, she said, "This is where Zander and Rafe sleep. There's a bunk bed in here, so there's room for another person. I'd like to think that one day, I'll have a full house with all the beds filled. The bathroom is right here," she motioned, showing him the big bathroom at the end of the hall.

"Now, for someone who is more afraid and would like some time alone, I have a smaller bedroom with a little bathroom attached, if you would prefer. I want you to be comfortable."

He peeked into that room, a single bed and dresser taking up the space. He could see a small sink and toilet through the door on the other side of the room. Staring, he considered his options. *This room would let me be by myself, but...* Glancing back down the hall, he spied Zander peering around the corner of the stairs, his eyes piercing but a grin on his face. Zander pointed a finger at his chest, opened his eyes wider, and his smile became bigger.

Taking a chance, Cael realized he did not want to be alone. Looking up at Miss Ethel, he said, "I'd like to be in the room with Zander and Rafe, if that's okay."

"Of course, it is," she exclaimed, taking his suitcase into the room.

He caught Zander's celebratory fist bump in the air, and his heart lightened for the first time in days.

As Miss Ethel tucked the twins in their beds across the hall, Cael sat on his bed, already comfortable with Zander and Rafe. Holding his bear, which he was thankful the other boys did not try to take, he listened as Zander read from a large storybook, skipping around to different stories.

Landing on Snow White, Zander laughed as he read the parts of the seven dwarfs in a silly voice. When he read the part of the Evil Queen, Cael's eyes grew wide and he snuggled under the covers. Miss Ethel entered the room, ready to tuck the boys into bed. She smiled widely, seeing Zander reading but, with a glance at Cael, she crossed to his bed, sitting next to him.

"Remember, sweet boy, fairy tales are wonderful... not because they tell us that evil exist, but because they tell us that evil can be beaten. So, listen to Zander's stories, but don't be afraid. For all my boys are brave." With a kiss each, she turned out the light, leaving on the nightlight.

He watched her leave, then turned his eyes to Zander, still reading. He listened to the story as long as he could, but exhausted, he soon fell asleep. With his bear tucked close, he slept all night while princes and princesses filled his dreams.

Sixteen-year-old, Cael stood in front of the mirror, staring at himself. Zander came up behind him and laughed.

"Damn, you look good in a monkey suit."

Throwing a glare his way, he tugged at the tie strangling his neck. The black tux had to be altered because he had left his gangly pre-teen body behind and was now filling out, resembling the pictures he had of his father when he was younger.

"Now, Zander, leave him alone," Miss Ethel gently scolded. "He looks handsome." Cael turned to face her and she placed her thin hand on his chest, smoothing his lapel. "It's an exciting day for your sister and I want you to have a good time. After her wedding, there will be the reception—"

"Where you'll have to dance with her," Rafe cut in, a grin on his face.

"Boys."

Immediately he and Zander threw their hands up in waves and headed back down the stairs, done with their teasing.

"Yes," she continued, "there will be dancing. And you'll be just fine."

"Is it weird that I'll be giving her away?" he asked, his brow creased with worry. "Won't people think I'm too young?"

"My dear, we're never too young to fulfil the roles we are meant to play. Your father's not alive and so, as the closest male relative, you will do the honor. And, you will not only make your sister very happy, but you'll make me so proud as well." She patted his chest and walked downstairs, leaving him to finish getting ready.

A few minutes later, as he prepared to walk out the front door, still nervous, she called out as she came up behind him, "Remember, family is everything, and your sister needs you today. You're very important to her, just as you are very important to us."

Turning, he offered her a hug. "Thank you, Miss Ethel—"

"You don't need to thank me, dear. There's no thanks needed among family. We'll be here when you get home, so go and have a good time."

With those words ringing in his ears, he headed to the car.

Cael hurried into the hospital, anxious to greet his sister and meet his new niece. Honorably discharged from the Army just one week earlier, at age twenty-two, he had made it to Richmond yesterday, enjoying the reunion at Miss Ethel's house.

Zander, also discharged, had bought a bar he appropriately named Grimm's. Jaxon and Jayden were still in the Army and had helped Zander get the bar in shape on one of their leaves. Rafe would be home in another few weeks, but his life was about to take a drastic turn. Having been photographed as Mr. July in an Army Hunk calendar, Rafe would be returning to modeling contracts that would send him out to California.

Cael grinned at the thought of Rafe, the model, not envying him at all. He would be starting a construction job next week, anxious to work with his hands. He had promised Zander he would help him finish the last work necessary for Grimm's opening, but with the early arrival of his niece, he wanted to spend as much time as he could bonding with his sister.

Walking past the nurse's station, he caught their wide-eyed expressions as they looked up at him. He was used to that reaction. At six feet seven inches and over two-hundred pounds of muscle, he knew that he was an imposing sight. He had not shaved since discharged and the week of scruff on his face gave him a harder appearance.

Entering the room, he saw her sitting in bed, dark circles underneath her eyes, but they twinkled with excitement. Stalking over, he skidded to a stop, seeing the little pink bundle in her arms. His mouth opened, but no words came out as his heart skipped a beat. The tiny rosebud mouth, dot of a nose, and squinty eyes held his rapt attention.

"Hey, brother," Kathy said, "come meet Cynthia. We're going to call her Cindy."

He barely glanced at Tom, his brother-in-law, as he

moved forward, his hand automatically reaching out to touch the baby's petal soft cheek.

As Kathy lifted Cindy, he took the bundle in his arms, love pouring from his heart to the tiny baby, knowing instantly he would do anything to protect his little niece.

2

SEVEN YEARS LATER

Cael climbed down the ladder inside the former warehouse, the framing almost complete. The construction company he worked for had begun the restoration of a large warehouse near the river, dividing it into spacious condos. He was now working in one of them, framing the inner walls with two by fours. The electrician was coming tomorrow to work on the wiring, so he wanted to finish today. He needed to check the schedule because he thought the plumber was coming in as well. *Good. That'll give me a couple of days to get the windows in.*

"Cael!" a shout rang out. Looking over, he saw Terrance, his boss, walking into the condo he was working on.

"What's up?"

"Where you at?"

"Framing's done. Electrician tomorrow and maybe the plumber too. I figure I'll start on the windows."

"I need you to be in unit seven tomorrow. Electrician's done in there but Joe's wife just called and the baby is coming early. I'll have you finish his windows while the electrician and plumber are in this unit."

"No problem," he replied. Checking his watch, he saw it was almost quitting time. Packing up his tools he nodded a goodbye and headed down to where the others were loading their trucks and securing the warehouse for the evening.

Waving at his co-workers, he headed down the road, deciding to grab a drink at Grimm's. With traffic, it took almost thirty minutes to make it across town before he finally pulled into the parking lot. Glad to see it not overly crowded, he climbed down from his truck and walked into the bar.

Roscoe, one of the bouncers, greeted him as he walked in and he waved to the two bartenders, Joe and Charlene, both entertaining the customers sitting at the long bar. Seeing Zander coming from the back hall, he lifted his chin in greeting. They met at one of the tables to the side and Zander signaled for another server to bring drinks.

"You get finished a little early?"

"Yeah. Boss cut us out about fifteen minutes early today since we had completed what needed to be done." Looking around, he said, "I guess I got here before the others."

"They'll be here," Zander replied, his eyes moving over the bar making sure everything was under control. Suddenly, the lines from his eyes deepened and his lips curved.

Without even looking he knew who must have entered. Turning slightly, he grinned at Rosalie as she made her way toward them. She kissed Zander as he jumped up to greet her, then settled into the chair next to him. They had recently gotten married in a quiet ceremony in Miss Ethel's backyard. Even though they hadn't been dating that long, Zander was not about to waste time on a long engagement and they married soon after she moved in with him.

"How's your sister?" Rosalie asked, her bright smile warm and friendly.

"She's good. Taking my niece back to the doctor today. Cindy hasn't been feeling very good lately. I should be hearing from them soon."

"I know children get sick often. I might work in a high school, but even the older kids are always sick."

The sound of the door slamming open had them turning around, observing as Jaxon and Jayden headed their way, with Asher right behind. Just as they reached the table, Rafe and Eleanor walked in as well.

The group greeted each other and, when the server brought pitchers of beer for the table, Zeke showed up with a large platter of wings.

Cael took a big bite and nodded toward Zeke. "Man, these are good. Glad grumpy here let you start cooking."

The group laughed and even Zander had to admit that turning the bar into a pub that served food had been a good idea. Zeke was one of Miss Ethel's boys who had showed up when Cael was already a teenager, but he had fit in well with them all and now worked for Zander. Asher, a year younger than the twins, had come to Miss Ethel's the year after Cael arrived. Other boys had come as well, but this group had stayed the tightest.

"How's your house coming?" Rafe asked.

"Good," he answered. "I've been working in the kitchen now and have almost finished. Ripped out the cabinets and counters. Got some leftover pieces from my work site that my boss is letting me have for next to nothing. I got the counters replaced and will get the new cabinets in soon."

"You gonna resell when you're finished?" Jaxon asked.

Shaking his head, he replied, "I don't know. I really like this house."

"It's not big enough for a family, the way it is," Eleanor pointed out. "I mean, I know you don't need that now, but someday you might."

"Yeah, definitely, for now, it's just me," he laughed. "But, I've started work on my plans to expand anyway. While I've been working on the kitchen, I've had a crew start on the extension in the back. They did the basic framing, wiring, plumbing, and insulation." Grinning, he added, "As soon as I get the kitchen finished, I'll call on y'all to help with the rest of the extension."

The conversation flowed among the friends as the servers kept the food and drinks coming.

His phone vibrated in his pocket and, pulling it out, he saw he had a text from his sister. **Need to talk but can't talk now. Will call later.**

His brow knit and Rosalie looked over, asking, "Is everything alright?"

"I guess so. My sister said she'll call me later 'cause she can't talk at the moment."

"Your niece is probably grumpy from her doctor visit."

Nodding politely, he felt his phone vibrate again. This time it was a text from his brother-in-law. **You're needed...as soon as possible.**

Jumping up, he said, "Sorry, I've got to go. Tom's just texted and said that I'm needed. Makes me think that something's happening and Kathy isn't handling it very well."

With hasty goodbyes and promises to let them know what was happening, he rushed out the door.

———

Sitting alone on a chair in Kathy and Tom's living room, Cael's leg bounced up and down at a rapid pace. He waited anxiously while the couple was upstairs putting Cindy to bed. By the time he had fought through the traffic to get to their house, they were with her and he did not want to interrupt the nighttime routine. After a few more minutes of nervous twitching, they walked down the stairs, their arms around each other.

One look at his sister's face and he knew something was wrong. Swallowing in an attempt to not choke on his fear, he remained quiet as they sat on the sofa, their hands clasped together.

Kathy took a deep breath before speaking. "Cindy's doctor found an enlarged lymph node at her last regular appointment. She's been feeling tired lately and has had a bit of a weight loss, which in seven-year-olds is unusual." She sighed and Tom tightened his hold on her.

"He ordered blood work and today told us that he wants her to have a needle biopsy, later this week, of the enlarged lymph node on her neck. He can't make a diagnosis until that's done, but he has let us know that he's checking to see if she has Lymphoma."

He sat perfectly still during her recitation, his focus centered on her. As her eyes lifted to his, his narrowed in confusion. "Okay," he said slowly. "What is that exactly?"

"It's a type of cancer," Tom said, looking from him to Kathy as she inhaled a shuddering breath.

Though still as a statue on the outside, Cael's heart began beating so hard he was surprised it managed to stay in his chest. Kathy appeared to be hanging on by a thread and Tom did not appear to be much better. *Calm...stay calm.* "I'm sure he's just preparing you for the worst..." his voice trailed off, his heart not feeling his words.

Standing quickly, he moved to the sofa and dropped to his knees, placing his hands over both of theirs. "Whatever you need...honest to God, whatever...I'm here for you and for her."

Kathy fell into his arms, her tears finally falling and he wrapped her tightly in his embrace. Looking over her head at Tom, his brother-in-law's tears undid him and he felt a slash of fear stabbing through him.

After several minutes, Kathy leaned back, wiping her face, a wobbly smile curving her lips. "I'm glad you're here, Cael."

"Me too, sis. Can I go up and just peek at her?" Gaining their nods, he rose and quietly tip-toed up the stairs. He was a large man, but his years in the Army had taught him how to move stealthily. His hand stilled on her door, partially opened since she was afraid of the dark, before he pushed it fully open, allowing the hall light to fall across the bed, illuminating Cindy.

Stepping toward her, his heart stumbled again. Her small frame was tucked underneath her bedspread with its Disney Tangled motif. Smiling, he had lost count of how many times he had sat and watched the movie with her. Bending over, he stared at her pale complexion, her face soft in slumber and watched as her breath came slow and even. Her hair flowed over the pillow and he reached out to touch the tresses. Cindy had his hair and knew it came from his father. The reddish-blonde strands were soft to his calloused fingertips.

Lymphoma. Cancer. Oh, Jesus, help us. He blinked away the tears that stung the backs of his eyes. Bending further, he placed a kiss on her cheek before moving back to the door. With a final goodbye whispered into the night, he walked back downstairs.

3

One week later, Cael walked into the Children's Hospital in Richmond. Stopping at the entrance, he closed his eyes for a moment to gather his wits. He had spent the past days convincing himself that Cindy was not really sick so, when the call came in today from Kathy, he felt blindsided. Quickly telling his boss he had to get to the hospital, he ran to his car and rushed there.

Sucking in a cleansing breath, he opened his eyes and moved to the reception desk. Giving his name and then getting his picture taken for the sticker ID, he followed a volunteer to the elevator. "I'm sure I can find my way," he said to the diminutive, elderly woman walking with him.

Smiling up, she said, "It's hospital policy to escort visitors until we get parental permission for them to have a recurring ID badge."

Stunned, he nodded silently, following her into the elevator. "Uh…is security always this high?"

She patted his arm, having to lean way back to

stare into his face. "It's a strange age we live in, and we take the security and privacy of our patients very seriously."

Oddly comforted, in spite of her lack of physical strength compared to his, he smiled down at her. "Then, I thank you for your diligence."

The elevator pinged their arrival on the third-floor and they stepped out together. Tom was waiting and signed the form for the volunteer to take back down. "Mr. Holland, it was nice to meet you. The next time you come in you can pick up your recurring ID. Just remember to bring your photo ID for it to be assigned to you." With that, she toddled down the hall.

Turning to Tom, he lifted his brow and Tom shook his head.

"I know, Cael. All I could think about is she looked like she would blow over in a strong wind and here she was escorting one of the biggest men I know."

He watched as Tom chuckled and figured the man needed a moment of mirth to cut through the agony they were facing. When Tom quieted, he asked gently, "What do I need to know before I go in there?"

Taking a deep breath before blowing it out heavily, he said, "She goes in for surgery tomorrow morning to remove the lymph node. From all indications, the Lymphoma is confined to the one node at this time. That's good news. And they are calling it Stage One. That's also good news. They are calling it a non-Hodgkins Lymphoma, which doesn't mean much to me, but supposedly it's easier to treat. The doctors are very optimistic, but I gotta tell you, Kathy's having a rough time. She's so great with Cindy and then falls apart at home."

He nodded, listening carefully to everything Tom was saying, once more with his heart pounding out of his chest. Blowing out a breath, he said, "I'm trying to take this all in, Tom. So, the bad news is Cindy has… fuck…she has…cancer." The word was pulled out of him and he hated hearing it on his own lips. Forcing his mind to focus, he continued, "But it looks good, overall."

"Yeah, that's about it for now."

"And the surgery'll take care of it? They can take it out and it's done?"

Tom's eyes cut away and he pinched the bridge of his nose with his forefinger and thumb before a tear slid down his cheek. "No…she'll have to have chemo as well."

Cael locked his knees in place to keep from dropping to the floor. "Oh, fuck no," he said, his voice barely a whisper. Blowing out his shaky breath, hands on his hips, he dropped his chin to his chest, his pounding heart now aching. Pulling himself together, he lifted his head and reached for Tom, offering a comforting hug. "Okay, man, I'm good. I'm here for you all."

Tom wiped his eyes and said, "Kathy's in there and Cindy's excited to see you. We're telling her what we believe she can handle, in a way she understands, so she knows she has a lump that the doctors will take out while she's asleep. She seems fine with that information."

"Got it."

Together, they walked the short distance down the

hall, stopping briefly at the door, both inhaling a deep breath before pushing inside.

Cael's gaze took in the room in one swoop. The walls were painted a soft blue with a darker blue for the door and window trim. Several Disney pictures were hung on the walls, giving the room a cheerier feel than a typical hospital room. The medical equipment was visible, but he let out a sigh of relief that, for now, she was not hooked up to any machines. A window to the side overlooked the trees in the courtyard below and the sun shone through the blinds.

"Uncle Cael!" came a cry of glee from the bed. Cindy was sitting in the middle of her hospital bed, dressed in a pink gown, and was combing the hair of a doll in her lap. Kathy was perched on the edge of the bed and cast an uncertain smile his way.

Grinning widely, he stalked over, bending to kiss his niece, noting Tom leaned in to whisper to Kathy while Cindy was distracted. She nodded and he assumed Tom let her know that he knew what was happening.

Eyes back on his little niece, he smiled brightly. "Cindy-loo, whatcha doing in this big bed?"

"I've got a lump in my neck that's not supposed to be there," she said, scrunching her nose. "But, tomorrow, the doctors will make me go to sleep and they'll take it out. Mom says it'll be like Sleeping Beauty where I'll be magically asleep until one of them kisses me at the end and then I'll wake up."

"Well, I'll be here, sweetie, so maybe I can be the one to give you a wake-up kiss," he suggested.

She giggled, her blue eyes bright. A nurse entered,

greeting her. "Hi, Cindy. I'm just back to make sure you're doing okay."

He watched as her smile dropped from her face as she stared at the nurse. "Are you gonna stick me?" she asked, her chin quivering.

Cael's gut clenched, thinking of what she had already endured and what was coming.

"Not now, sweetie, but it's almost time for your supper, because in two hours you won't be able to eat until tomorrow. So, would you like chicken and mashed potatoes? We've got orange Jello also."

Cindy's face brightened and she nodded enthusiastically. Cael looked over at his sister and said, "I'd like to stay with her for a bit, so why don't you and Tom go downstairs to eat."

Shooting him a grateful smile, they kissed Cindy before walking out. He turned his attention back to her and said, "Look what I brought."

"Mr. Zander's book!"

"That's right. He loaned it to me so that we could read some while you eat."

The nurse returned with Cindy's dinner tray, setting it in front of her, and she began to eat delicately while he settled in the chair next to her bed, opening the story book. "What would you like?"

"Tinkerbell," she said while nibbling on her chicken.

"Ah, Peter Pan." Turning to the page, he read as she finished eating and pushed the tray away. After she settled down in the bed, he pulled the covers up over her. Her eyes became heavy and she clutched her doll to her chest as they finally closed. Kathy and Tom came back into the room, but he continued to read until he was sure she was almost asleep.

"You know that place between sleep and awake, the place where you can still remember dreaming? That's where I'll always love you. That's where I'll be waiting."

Closing the book, he stood, bent over her small body and whispered, "That's where I'll be waiting tomorrow. Sweet dreams."

Kissing her forehead, he turned to gather Kathy in his arms, kissing the top of her head. "Guys, I'll be here tomorrow. I've already cleared it with my boss. I'll take tomorrow off and then I'll also take other days off as we know what we're facing."

Once in the lobby, he shot a group text to Miss Ethel and the guys, letting them know what was happening. Shoving his phone into his pocket, he moved toward the door.

Walking out of the hospital and into the night, he sucked in a great gulp of cool air. Stopping at his truck, he placed his hands on the hood, leaning his head down as he grappled with his emotions. Four years in the Army, working construction with the Corps of Engineers, with tours in Afghanistan and he had never felt so out of control.

Lifting his head, he stared at the sky, now dotted with stars, and prayed about tomorrow.

Two weeks later, Cael finished working by three

o'clock. His boss had allowed him to shift his hours around so he arrived on the construction site at six a.m. and worked until three o'clock, earlier if he skipped lunch. This gave him the chance to spend the afternoons with Cindy, giving Kathy a break. Tom worked at home as a software consultant, so his hours could be flexible as well.

Saying goodbye to his boss, Terrance stopped him. "How's she doing?"

Shrugging, he said, "As good as can be expected. The surgery went well and the docs think they got all the cancer with the lymph node, so she's been home for over a week now and has recuperated really well. But, now she starts chemo. In fact, today was her first treatment and I'm heading over to the hospital."

"She gotta stay there?"

"For now, they want to monitor her and see how she does. They'll also run some tests constantly to see if they need to switch up her meds. She'll be in a controlled environment for a bit. They're really afraid of her getting sick, with the flu hitting the area so hard."

Clapping him on the back, Terrance said, "We're praying for her. My wife's got her prayer circle going, but I want you to take care of yourself as well. You're no good to your family if you get worn out."

"Thanks, boss."

"By the way, Cael, when things get better, I've got something I want to discuss with you. A kind of business proposal. But it'll wait. For now, focus on your family."

Curious, he nonetheless just nodded at Terrance and climbed into his truck.

The drive to the hospital was now so familiar he could make it in his sleep. Nonetheless, he rubbed the back of his neck hoping he didn't actually fall asleep at the wheel. Shaking that thought from his mind, he knew the fatigue he felt was nothing compared to the worry Kathy and Tom felt every second, or his sweet Cindy, whose body was fighting not only the cancer, but now the chemo as well.

Making it in good time, the trip was easy, with little traffic. Bolting out of the vehicle, he strode into the hospital, stopping to get his new badge, nodding toward the volunteers at the front desk. As the elevator let him off on the fifth floor this time, Tom met him. They quickly embraced before Tom showed him the prep station. Donning a gown and mask, he washed his hands with the antibacterial soap. Tom introduced him to the nurses at their station before they made their way to Cindy's room.

Entering, he plastered a smile on his face, both genuine, for seeing his niece, and insincere, because he hated to see her in this place. She was sitting in bed, this time dressed in a blue hospital gown with yellow ducks decorating it. Her strawberry-blonde hair was pulled back with a wide pink headband. It had been cut and now hung just below her ears. Dark circles were underneath her eyes and he swore she seemed thinner than the day before. He saw the IV line snaking under the top of her gown and swallowed hard. Grinning as she saw him, he headed directly to her. Wanting to kiss her, he chose to touch his mask-covered lips to the top of her head instead.

"How's my favorite girl?" he asked.

She wrinkled her nose and said, "So-so. Are you going to read to me?"

"Absolutely," he promised. He glanced to the side and added, "I'm gonna talk to your mom for a few minutes and then we'll read, okay?"

He walked to the door with Kathy and asked in hushed tones, "What can you tell me?"

Shrugging, she lifted her tired eyes to him and replied quietly, "The doctors think it's going well, but she immediately got sick after the treatment. She threw up and has barely kept anything down since. They have her on fluids and other meds, including an anti-nausea."

She looked over at Cindy, playing with a doll, and placed her fingers to her lips to stop their trembling. "They say she'll probably lose her hair."

Gasping, he blinked. *Of course...why didn't I think of that possibility?* Forcing his mind back to Kathy, he shook his head sadly, saying, "I'm sorry, sis."

"I know it's so stupid to be upset over her hair when it's her life that's being saved. She always loved her hair, but was so brave when we cut it short today to make it easier during her hospital stays. Now, she'll probably lose it all."

Placing his hands on her shoulders, he pulled her in for a hug. "You and Tom go get some dinner. Get out of the hospital and go to a real restaurant. I'll stay until you get back and we'll be fine. I brought a few more books to read to her."

"Cael...I don't know how to thank you. I honestly don't think that we could be doing this without—"

"No thanks needed, sis. We're family...if there's one thing Miss Ethel always taught us guys, it was that family comes first."

With a small smile, she nodded, said goodbye to Cindy, and then walked out the door.

Turning to Cindy when they were alone, he asked, "So, what shall we read tonight?"

Grinning, she pointed to a pile of books on the shelf. "Tangled. Dad brought some of my books from home."

Picking up the well-worn Disney book, he said, "We've read this book so many times, you have it memorized."

"But I love it," she exclaimed. He bent to pull up the chair, but she said, "No, Uncle Cael, you can sit on my bed."

"Honey, I don't think your bed will hold me."

Laughing, she said, "You are big. You might break it, just like in Goldilocks!"

Chuckling, he settled in the chair and they read together. She soon became sleepy and he encouraged her to slide underneath the covers, tucking them around her once she was lying down.

"Uncle Cael," her soft voice sounded, her large eyes staring at him. "If my hair goes away, like the princess' in Tangled, will it hurt?"

His heart squeezed in his chest as he blinked at the tears in his eyes. "No, baby, it won't hurt. And it'll grow back again."

"Promise?"

"I promise," he vowed. As her eyes closed he continued to read, though his voice was choked with emotion.

"And when I promise something, I never break that promise."

Standing, he kissed her head once more as Kathy entered the room. "I promise," he whispered.

4

Sitting in the living room of Miss Ethel's house, Cael leaned against the cushions on the sofa, his gaze roaming over the familiar setting. The room was comfortably furnished with a dark green sofa, colorful throw pillows against the back. The wooden end tables were covered in white, crocheted lace. A thick rug warmed the center of the wooden floor and two deep cushioned chairs sat facing the sofa, one always used by Miss Ethel, her knitting bag at her feet. The walls on either side of the fireplace held bookshelves, filled with children's books.

Her knitting needles clicked continuously but her eyes were on him. Zander sat in the other chair, Rosalie in his lap. Rafe was on one end of the sofa, with Eleanor in his lap, and Asher sat in the middle, next to him. Jaxon and Jayden had brought in dining room chairs for themselves. Zeke made himself comfortable on the floor, his back against Miss Ethel's chair.

The gathering had listened as he talked about

Cindy's treatment and how Kathy and Tom were doing, each expressing their concerns.

"She's awfully brave," he admitted, "but she's got weeks more treatments to go."

"If they think they got it all with surgery, why does she have to have chemo?" Jaxon asked.

"I'm not really sure. Honestly, it's been hard to focus on anything other than Cindy and how she is doing. When the doctors and nurses explain things it's like I'm hearing it through a tunnel." He wiped his face with his hands and leaned back, breathing deep.

Eleanor looked at him sympathetically and offered, "I'm not an oncologist, but we were required to learn some things when I was studying to become a nurse. Basically, doctors don't want to take a chance that they might have missed something. The surgery removed the cancer that they're sure of, but cancer cells can travel through the lymph system so easily. The chemo, and possible radiation, will help to ensure that they get it all."

"But isn't the treatment worse for such a little child than it is for an adult?" Rosalie asked, her eyes full of sorrow.

Eleanor observed the haggard expression on his face that matched those of everyone in the room, before answering what they all were concerned about. "I know it seems that way, but if they feel that it was at stage one, then there's a really good chance that she can be cancer free."

Rafe asked, "Stage one?"

"Of the four stages, one is the least severe. It's where

the Lymphoma is at one site, generally nodal, but not in the chest or abdomen."

The gathering sighed in unison and Cael rubbed his hand over his face again.

"Dear boy, you all have been through so much." Miss Ethel lay her needles down and continued, "I have already called Kathy and told her that I can sit with them tomorrow. You need to take a break."

"No. I can't—"

"You can and you will," she pronounced. Holding his gaze, her eyes warm on him, she added, "You need to let us help you and, by doing so, you give us the chance to give to your family as well."

"When was the last time you went out and did something just for you?" Asher asked.

As Cael started to protest, Miss Ethel shook her head. "No, it's important for you to take care of you. You cannot take care of your family if you're worn to a frazzle."

Nodding slowly, he said, "Thank you." Standing, he offered his goodbyes, hugs given all around. As he was about to head out the door, Rosalie left Zander's side and moved to him. Lifting on her toes, he bent so she could kiss his cheek. Still close, she whispered, "Go out. Have a drink tonight, Cael." Grinning, she added, "Go hook up. Have some fun. Take some time just for you."

Chuckling, he gave her a quick hug and walked to his truck. Driving down the road, he hesitated at the intersection, when his phone vibrated.

After seeing who it was he answered in a rush. "Sis? Is everything alright?"

"Yes and no. Cindy is okay for now but several cases of the flu have hit some of the patients and the hospital is not taking any chances. They aren't letting in any visitors other than parents and guardians for a few days. Sorry, but you can't come over until it's cleared."

"Fuck, sis. I'm sorry. Miss Ethel was going to come tomorrow."

"I know. I'm going to call her next. She wanted to bring some food to Tom and me anyway, so I can see her then, she just can't come up to Cindy."

Sighing heavily, he said, "Give Cindy a kiss for me and tell her I'll be there the first day they let me back in."

Hanging up, he didn't to go home, but he also did not want to go to Grimm's. The desire for a drink, somewhere he was not known, had him turning in a different direction, toward the downtown bars.

The music blared from the speakers hung in the corners as Cael watched people dancing on the floor near the back of the bar. Not his usual place to visit, he nonetheless enjoyed the anonymity of drinking here, without anyone wondering why he was drowning his worries. He had switched from beer to whiskey, but with his size and the full meal he had at Miss Ethel's, he was far from officially drunk...more like officially relaxed.

Sitting on a stool at the end of the bar with his back against the wall, he stared over the crowd. The men were wandering around, eyes on the women dancing. The women were plentiful, dressed to impress, more than a few of which were on the prowl. A big man, he drew attention to himself, even sitting.

A few women had approached him for a dance but he preferred to watch for now. He had also turned down several offers to go home with someone, but now wondered why he had. It had been awhile since he had gone home with someone for sex. And he always left after the sex. Spending the night with someone indicated a level of intimacy he had not found yet. *Sex for a night, with a stranger, sounds just like what I need.*

Standing to stretch his legs he was able to easily observe the crowded room, bodies moving around. A flash of color crossed his vision and he blinked, willing his eyes to focus. Looking down the bar, a woman was standing with her back to him, tall, with a great ass in a tight pair of jeans. Her hair, though, that was what really drew him in. The thick, silky tresses hung down in soft waves to the middle of her back. The length alone would have snagged his attention, but the color enraptured him. The reddish-blonde strands appeared to glisten like copper and gold in the lights of the bar, shimmering with each movement her body made.

His feet propelled him forward of their own volition until he was directly behind her. Now close, he could see that the strands were actually multi-colored... yellow, gold, red, auburn. All combined to give the effect of a magical halo floating around her. Shaking his head in wonder, he peered down at her, seeing that, while she was tall, she was also wearing heels, bringing her head to where it would just tuck under his chin.

Her right hand was resting on the bar, long fingers and perfectly manicured nails tapping in time to the music on the wooden surface. A sudden image of her hands on him caused a jolt to shoot through him and his cock twitched. She was alone, but staring toward the back of the bar. He looked in the direction she was staring but did not see anyone she might be with.

The bartender sat a drink on the bar, making a witty comment, and she threw her head back in laughter, turning just enough that he could view her profile. Porcelain skin with a smattering of light freckles across her classic nose. Her cheeks held a rosy glow and her summer-sky blue eyes were framed with thick lashes, darker than her hair. Lips with a hint of pink gloss captured his gaze and the desire to taste them had his breath leaving his lungs in a rush. Giving his head another shake, he could not remember the last time he had such a visceral reaction to a woman.

Just then she turned to take a drink, lifting the glass to her lips, when she caught sight of him and jolted. Her gaze landed on his massive chest and a gasp left her lips. Her eyes widened as she slowly lifted them, finally leaning her head back a bit in an effort to see his face. Before she had a chance to speak, his lips curled and his face relaxed into a friendly smile.

"Hey, beautiful," he said, unable to think of another greeting.

Cocking her head to the side, she met his grin with one of her own. "Is that your best pick-up line?"

Chuckling, he shook his head slowly. "Just calling it like I see it and you are the most beautiful woman I've ever seen. In. My. Life."

Regina's mouth opened, but the quick retort died on her lips. She stared at the handsome mountain of a man standing in front of her. At five feet, eight inches, she usually stared men in the eye when wearing heels, but this man made her feel small. He had to be six and a half feet tall and had more muscles than she had ever seen. Eyes roving his body discretely, at first, his wide shoulders and thick arms filled out the navy shirt he wore, the rolled sleeves straining at the seams.

Her gaze traveled down the length of him, blatantly now, taking her time. His waist tapered to trim hips, his jeans fitting perfectly. The crotch was well worn and his thick thighs filled the denim material. His large, heavy boots were the perfect ending to an exquisite masculine package.

Licking her lips, she allowed her eyes to slowly lift, taking him in again. "Wow, you must be a Brobdingnagian." A sly, secret smile curved her lips as she began to turn away, lifting her drink to her lips and taking a healthy gulp.

Rising to the challenge, he replied, "So you think that Jonathan Swift had me in mind when he wrote Gulliver's Travels?"

Her eyes widened and her smile broadened. "A well-read man. Now that is sexy," she purred.

Quoting Gulliver, he said, "'My hours of leisure I spent in reading the best authors, ancient and modern, being always provided with a good number of books.'"

Her smile morphed into a full-blown grin as she finished the quote, "And when I was ashore, in observing the manners and dispositions of the people, as well as learning their language; wherein I had a great facility, by the strength of my memory."

"Damn, Red. A witty, smart, and gorgeous woman. Talk about sexy."

Tapping her finger on her chin, she declared, "I think I'll call you Titan. That's easier than Brobdingnagian. You're definitely more than just a giant...you're more of a mythical warrior."

Shifting his stance closer, causing her to lift her chin higher to keep her eyes on him, he replied, "Maybe I should call you Lili—"

"Hey, I'm not a Liliputian, as you can clearly see," she retorted as her hand made a swoop down her body. "I'm hardly short...well, unless standing next to a Titan."

At her invitation, Cael's gaze traveled slowly down the front of her, gloriously displayed for his perusal. Firm breasts filled out her green sweater. Her trim waist led to the soft curves of her hips, showcased in tight jeans. Her feet, encased in open-toed heels, gave evidence to red-painted toenails. Entirely understated sexy, he reached out his hand to her shoulder to brush her hair back, his fingers feeling a spark underneath their tips at the first touch.

"I think I'll stick to Red."

Regina sucked in a shuddering breath, unable to remember the last time she was so affected by a man's presence. "Titan and Red. I like that."

"Nicknames only?" Cael asked, noting the flash of hardness that cooled her green eyes.

"Yes…for whatever is happening tonight…nicknames only. No names and no regrets."

"A woman after my own heart."

She shook her head slowly, the coolness in her eyes replaced with a hint of pain. "No…I'm not after anyone's heart."

Sliding his hand down her arm until it came to her hand, he lifted it while glancing at her ring finger. *No engagement or wedding ring. No indentation where one might have been.*

Interpreting his perusal, she said, "Not married. Not engaged. Just a free woman out enjoying herself at a bar. Some drinks. Some dancing. And if I happen to meet someone interesting, I'm free to do what I want."

"Just Red?"

"That's me…just Red."

"So, tell me something about Just Red. What else do you like to read other than Gulliver's Travels?"

"Would you believe me if I said I love historical novels?" Seeing his eyes widen, Regina said, "Honest to God, I love anything about the Elizabethan period."

"Britain…sixteenth century?"

"Oh, my, a man who knows his history. Now you really are sexy!" she laughed.

"My preference is before that…War of the Roses."

She stared at him, before swinging her gaze around, her eyes narrowing as she searched the area.

Cocking his head to the side, he asked, "What are you looking for?"

"A hidden camera."

"Huh?"

Her smile widened as she brought her gaze back to his. "This must be some kind of hidden reality show, because there's no way a random guy meets me and likes the same obscure things I do!"

Cael threw his head back in laughter, feeling lighter than he had in weeks. "Damn, Red. You are too good to be true."

Taking her empty glass from her, he sat it on the bar and linked his fingers with hers, feeling both warmth and strength. Stepping around her, he drew her with him, toward the dance floor.

Regina followed willingly, her hand firmly in his, allowing him to lead. A strange sense of rightness passed over her. *What the hell...I've got nothing to lose.* Once they were immersed in the crowd, he swung her around and she landed flush against his chest. One of his large hands spanned the small of her back, holding her close, his fingertips barely touching the top of her ass. The hand that was linked with hers was pressed to their fronts, close to his heart.

The music caused their feet to move and just before Cael thought he might drown in her eyes, he swung her out and then, as she came back, he stepped behind her, the feel of her ass against his crotch sweet torture. She laughed, grinding herself against him, the power in her moves heady. Hands in the air, she gyrated to the beat, clearly loving the feel of his body moving in time with hers.

"You've got the moves, Red," he whispered in her ear, just loud enough for her to hear over the music.

Twisting her head around, she grinned up at him. "Aww, Titan. I'm just getting started." Whipping around, she faced him, her hands on his shoulders. The strength of his muscles underneath her fingertips caused her to dig them in slightly, testing just how firm they were. He was easily the largest man she had ever been this close to, but she felt nothing but safe with him. Biting her lip, she wondered how far she was willing to go tonight.

"Glad to hear it, Red, cause this night's gonna blow your mind."

Laughing again, she slid her hands around his neck and pressed in tighter to his front. On cue, the music changed to a slow melody and their bodies reacted accordingly. His arms tightened around her trim frame and she rested her head on his shoulder. As the lights glistened and the music cocooned them, the rest of the crowd faded away.

With her sweet body next to his, Cael found his breath caught in his throat, his heart pounding. Something was happening and he had no idea what it was. *She's just a woman. Just like any other woman I've picked up in a bar.* Regardless what his mind argued, his arms reacted, pulling her even closer.

She felt the pressure of his arms around her and lifted her head. Her quip died on her lips as she stared at the intense expression on his face. Without thinking, one hand slid up to cup his strong cheek and her thumb caressed his full lips.

Cael growled, slamming his lips onto hers, capturing her mouth in a firm kiss, long and wet. She reacted immediately, opening her mouth to allow his probing tongue access. Taking her invitation, he plunged his tongue inside her warmth, searching out each crevice as the sensations shot straight to his cock. There was a groan, but for all he could tell it could have come from either of them.

God, this man can kiss. Breathless, she still did not come up for air, not caring if she died right there in his arms.

Their heads moved back and forth as their noses bumped, both trying to dominate the kiss. She cupped the back of his head, fingertips sliding through his short, light red hair, angling him the way she wanted. His day-old stubble abraded her skin but she welcomed the slight sting. Not used to making out with a stranger —or anyone—in the middle of a bar, she nonetheless was unable to back away, even if his hand had not been clamped to the middle of her back, holding her close.

After a minute, she felt lightheaded from the heat but, whether it was from the crowd or the partner, she was not sure. "Think I need a break," she gasped, hoping he would not be disappointed.

His eyes registered concern and he immediately led her to a table in the corner where the music was less loud. Signaling to a server, he turned to her and asked, "Water?" Obtaining her nod, he gave the order to the woman who came by. Settling next to her, his eyes still pinned on her, he said, "You okay, Red?"

Blushing, she swiped her hand over her forehead and nodded. "Sorry, I just felt really hot all of a sudden."

The server brought the water and she drank greed-ily. She caught his worried expression and assured, "I'm fine, honestly." Shoulder bumping him, she said, "I just needed to get out of the crowd."

His gaze dropped to her mouth as her tongue darted out to moisten her lips. Seeing where his attention had moved to, and knowing he was now cautious, she leaned in, making the first move, desperate for his kiss again.

Cael wrapped his arm around her back, pulling her in close once more. He had wondered if the power of the first kiss was a fluke, brought on by the music and full body contact. But with the feel of her body next to his again, he once more became lost in her taste. His hand slid through her thick, silken hair, fingers tangling in the tresses. He could not remember the last time he had been so enthralled with a woman's hair and his mind flamed with the desire to see it curtained around them when she was naked, on top, riding him.

Regina melted into his arms, tangling her hands in his hair before sliding them over his shoulders. The play of muscles under his shirt captured her attention and the desire to run her fingers over his naked body flamed her imagination. She wanted this kiss, this man, more than anything. *Well, almost more than anything.* Now wasn't the time for that though, so she cast the thought to the recesses of her mind. *I want this...this night, just for me.*

As though he could hear her thoughts, the good ones not the bad, he dragged his lips from hers. His ragged breathing matched hers and he no longer seemed to care if he did not represent the suave man-about-town, rather appearing more like a hungry man being presented with a feast. And she was all in for that.

Looking into her hooded eyes, all Cael wanted was one night to forget about anything else but her body with his. *One night just to forget my worries.*

"Red…" he started, his rough voice unfamiliar to his ears.

"Yes," she replied to his unanswered question. Seeing his eyes narrow in uncertainty, she swallowed deeply before continuing. "Yes. I want you. Tonight. All of you."

Nodding, he took her hand and they stood but, instead of heading out, they remained completely still, gazes locked, while the crowd moved around them. Sucking in a shaky breath, she pleaded, "Please, Titan. I'll beg if I have to."

A smile curved his lips as he leaned in, whispering in her ear, "You'll never have to beg me, darlin'." Straightening, he linked his fingers with hers and said, "Come on, Red."

He moved swiftly and she willingly followed. It might be unwise to allow a stranger to pull her along, but the gentle touch of his hand felt so right. Tired of playing it safe, she threw caution to the wind and allowed him to lead her into the cool, dark night.

5

Stopping at his truck, Cael whirled Red around, fingers still linked, and backed her up against the door. He wanted to press his aching cock into her soft body again, but halted a few inches away. Looking down, he held her gaze. "Who do you need to call?"

Titan's deep voice slid over Regina, melting her so that it took her a moment to realize he had asked a question. Her mouth opened but no words came out as her brows lowered in confusion.

"A friend? Someone you can tell where you are and who you're with." When she continued to ponder his question silently, he added, "Red, you're a woman about to go off with a man you don't know. Make sure someone knows."

"We agreed—no names tonight. I want to stick to that." His lips pinched, determined, so she quickly pulled out her phone. "Hey," she said softly when they answered. "Just letting you know I'm going to—" she halted as she peered up at him.

"Richmond Hilton...downtown."

Lifting an eyebrow with a half-smile on her face, she repeated, "The Richmond Hilton. As soon as I get there, I'll let you know what room I'm in." She listened before laughing, "Of course, I know what I'm doing." After another moment, she finished with, "All right, good-night," and disconnected, sliding her phone back into her purse. "I'm not sure that makes a whole lot of sense telling my...uh, friend that I'm going to a hotel, since I can't give them a name, but I feel like throwing caution to the wind tonight." Stepping closer, pulling his body flush with hers, she urged, "Kiss me."

Smirking his satisfaction, Cael leaned the rest of the way in, pressing his body into hers so that they were touching from knee to head. Her breasts were against his chest, his cock flush with her stomach. He bent to take her lips, folding his body around hers protectively. Their lips moved over each other's, tongues dancing again. His cock swelled painfully and he wondered how he would managed to drive. Leaning back, he sucked in a deep breath.

"Gotta back off, Red, or I'll never make it to the hotel."

She licked her kiss-swollen lips and grinned. "Then let's go. I may be crazy, but I trust you."

"That's not crazy at all. I swear it." He tried to convey the truth and honesty of that statement in his eyes, looking deeply into hers. She nodded, slowly, and he acknowledged her understanding with a quick dip of his chin. "All right, then. Your carriage awaits." Shifting her out of the way, he opened her door and assisted her into his truck. Leaning over her chest, he fastened her seat belt, stealing another kiss at the same time. Rounding the front, he climbed into the driver's seat and started the engine, pulling out of the parking lot.

"Nice truck," she said, her face turned toward him.

"Thanks. Traded in my SUV when I really needed a pickup for hauling stuff."

Driving, he slid his hand over to her lap, linking fingers once more. Regina looked down at his hand, so large and rough compared to her much slimmer one. She knew he could crush her easily, but she felt nothing but ease in his presence. Glancing to the side at his strong profile, she smiled. *Just one night. I only want just one night.*

A few minutes later they walked into the Hilton, hand in hand. As they moved to the reception desk to check into the hotel, she noted the opulent lobby with red leather sofas and chairs in conversations areas and sleek modern chandeliers hanging above. To the right was the entrance to the bar, the sounds of clinking glasses and soft music flowing from the doorway. The connecting restaurant appeared to still be in full service despite the late hour. A hand on her lower back startled her and she jumped, looking behind her only to blush as she observed Titan smiling down at her.

"Ready?"

Meeting his smile, she nodded. "I was just admiring the lobby. I've never been here before."

"Me either," he replied, never taking his eyes off her.

Pondering his comment, the look on his face as he said it, like it meant something for her to know that, as he escorted her to the elevator, she turned once they entered and said, "We could have gone somewhere a lot cheaper. I mean, this is lovely, but..."

"Overdone for a one-night?" he finished for her.

A giggle slipped out. "Yeah..."

He moved into her space, keeping barely an inch between their bodies as the elevator ascended. "Can't explain it, Red. I don't do a lot of one-nighters and certainly not like this. But, there's something about you. Maybe it's 'cause you're sexy as hell and I want to do something special for you. Maybe it's 'cause you're witty and smart and I don't want you in some fleabag hotel."

Her eyes dancing with mirth, she agreed, "I wouldn't want to be in a fleabag hotel either."

"Maybe it's 'cause with all that's going on around me, I need this. You. Here. This. Tonight." He lifted one finger and traced the curve of her cheek, along her jaw, to her chin, where he lifted it slightly.

She sobered at his words and the look of need on his face. "Yeah," she breathed, thinking he had just described her feelings exactly.

The elevator doors opened and he pulled back, leaving her longing for the kiss that did not happen. Instead, he turned swiftly, leading her out by their linked hands again. As they approached the end of the hall, he said, "Send your text to your friend. Tell 'em we're in room 917."

She dispatched the text as he ordered and barely had

time to replace her phone in her purse when he had the door unlocked and she found herself lifted into his strong arms as he stalked inside the room.

Kicking the door closed with his boot, Cael turned quickly, placing Red's back against the door. Shifting her hips, she wrapped her legs around his waist, nestling her heated core against the bulge in his jeans. He felt the heat of her searing through their clothes and his cock swelled painfully.

His mouth slammed onto hers again, the force almost painful, but as his tongue invaded her mouth, Regina melted in his arms. Grabbing his jaw with both hands, she allowed him dominance over the kiss while holding him in place. He tasted of whiskey and man, a heady combination. She had several vodka cranberry cocktails at the bar, but was certain she was sober. She had never felt so alive. *Alive. God, yes, alive!*

Her breasts pressing against his chest and the feel of her soft ass in his hands drove all other thoughts from Cael's mind other than wanting to get her naked and underneath him. Or maybe against the door. Or maybe on the desk he observed for a brief second as he entered the room. Or maybe all of them. Suddenly, the idea of a one-and-done did not appeal. He wanted the whole night, at least, which was something he never did.

He felt a nip of teeth on his lips and jerked. "Hey," he mumbled, his lips still on hers.

She pushed his head back slightly and said, "Where did you go? You were kissing me but your head was somewhere else."

His eyes stayed on hers, a slow smile curving his lips. "I assure you, Red, my thoughts were on you. I was just thinking about our arrangement." Seeing her brows lower, he rushed, "I mean, I want the whole night. No slipping away after one time. I want you as many ways as I can get you and then, when we're sated, I want to sleep beside you all night. When the morning comes, I'll want you again. What do you say?"

"Hmmm," she hummed, pretending to be considering the idea. "That sounds like you'll need a lot of stamina."

"Stamina's never been a problem, babe."

"And condoms? You came prepared?" she asked, lifting her brow.

"I think I've got us covered."

"You think?"

"I know. And, if we happen to exceed my wildest expectations, there's a drug store next door to the hotel."

"Well, aren't you the boy scout, always prepared."

Barking out a laugh, he leaned back in, silencing her with his lips on hers again. Angling his head, he slid his tongue inside, tangling with hers, tasting the fruity drink she had been drinking when he first saw her.

Regina tightened her legs, pulling his crotch closer, the delicious heat from his cock striking her core through the denim barrier. She shifted, increasing the friction she craved. Groaning, she rubbed harder, sure she would be able to come just from dry humping.

He pushed back and she groaned louder, this time in discontent.

"When you come, Red, it'll be with us flesh on flesh."

Biting her lip, she grinned. Nodding, she slid her legs to the floor as he backed away slowly.

Linking fingers, Cael continued to back toward the bed, taking her along with him. As soon as his legs hit the mattress, he stopped. He slid his hands to the bottom of her sweater and, gaining her nod, lifted it over her head, observing it snag on her breasts before it passed over her head and landed onto the floor. Dropping his gaze, his breath caught in his throat at her breasts barely covered in a pale green, silk bra. Her breasts, not overly large, fit her curves perfectly.

She stood statue still, her eyes on his face. He placed his forefinger on the pulse point of her neck and slowly dragged it downward in the center of her chest until it snagged on the front closure of her bra. With a deft flick, he unfastened the slip of material and watched it flutter to the ground behind her.

Her perfect breasts bounced slightly at the movement, her rosy nipples now hard points, begging to be sucked. He lifted her easily in his arms, bringing the tempting buds to his mouth. Pulling one in deeply, he heard her moan as he sucked hard, nipping with his teeth as she threw her head back, arching her back and pushing her breasts into his face even more.

Leaving one nipple, he kissed his way to the other, sucking it just as deeply. More intoxicating than his earlier whiskeys, he flicked the extended flesh with his tongue. His cock ached painfully, straining against his zipper, but he wanted to savor each moment with her.

Twisting, he lay her back on the bed, crawling over

her. Her breasts were now slightly red from his beard and mouth. The sight of her nipples practically begging for attention made leaning away from them even harder. Hearing her small groan, he chuckled.

"I want you naked," he said, his hands at her jean's zipper. Making short work of unfastening them, he slid then down her long legs, snagging her pale green, silky panties at the same time. "Love the undies, Red."

"Wore 'em just for you," she quipped, loving the feel of being naked for his perusal.

"Smartass," he laughed, nipping her stomach before soothing it with a kiss.

"Aren't you a little overdressed," she complained, eyeing him eagerly. "You've unwrapped me like a present and I'd like to have a chance to do the same."

"All in good time. Right now, I've got you just the way I want you." Before she had a chance to complain about his high-handedness, Cael continued to kiss his way down her abdomen, over her neatly trimmed mound and, with a toss of her legs over his shoulders, he dove in, latching his mouth over her sex. The heat of her, the scent of her, the taste of her, all combined and he was undone. Afraid he would come in his pants like an untried teenager, he focused on her pleasure.

Delving his tongue inside her channel, he slowly licked up toward her clit, giving the swollen bud a tweak. Lifting his eyes to her face, he watched as her head slammed back against the mattress and her hands fisted the comforter. Sliding a finger into her sex, it was immediately coated with her moisture and he felt her inner muscles quiver. Quirking his finger, he hit the spot as he sucked her clit into his mouth deeper and she cried out, "Titan!"

A mixed emotion hit him. He loved bringing her to climax, yet longed to hear his real name on her lips. *No names, no regrets. Why does that suddenly not sound so good anymore?*

Her legs fell from his shoulders, bringing his thoughts back to the delicious taste on his lips. Kissing his way up her body, he paused to give each breast attention, before continuing on his path to her lips.

Groaning, Regina tasted herself on his tongue. Reaching down, she snagged the bottom of his shirt, attempting to pull it up. Struggling, she said, "You gotta help a girl out."

He laughed as he pulled back and stood between her legs. Reaching behind him, he grabbed the back of his shirt and pulled it over his head, dropping it at his feet.

She leaned up on her elbows, her chest heaving with each breath at the sight of him. His shoulders...chest... biceps...all massive. It was obvious he lifted weights but she got the feeling that he worked in a job that used those muscles too. She started to ask, but halted. *No personal information.* Starting to regret their agreement, she stayed quiet, allowing her gaze to peruse down his washboard abs and focus on his hands at his belt. It slid from the loops before he unzipped his pants. His erection was so prominent, his boxers tented as soon as the zipper was undone. *Jesus, he's big. All over...big.*

Clearing her throat as he dropped his jeans and boxers and stood there in all his naked glory, fisting his cock, she said, "Please."

"Told you, Red. You don't gotta beg." He bent to grab his wallet from his jean's pocket and pulled out a strip of condoms. Ripping open one, he tossed the others onto the nightstand.

As he rolled it on his cock, she grinned, "Boy Scout."

Crawling onto the bed, he nudged her legs apart and said, "Damn, girl, you're just begging to be spanked."

Her core clenched at his words. She knew he could tell she had a physical reaction when he laughed.

"Shut up and get in me," she ordered, spreading her legs wide for him and wrapping her feet around his waist.

His eyes darkened with lust and he plunged in with one forceful push. He halted as she gasped, looking down, concern on his face.

Shaking her head back and forth, she breathed, "Keep going. It's okay...I just...God, you're big."

It was not the first time Cael had heard a woman make that claim but coming from her lips, it affected him in an unfamiliar way. Before, it had seemed more as a woman coyly stroking his ego or, perhaps, to gain bragging rights to her girlfriends later. But, from Red's lips, it was almost spoken reverently.

"I want you comfortable," he whispered, watching her closely.

"Move...please just move," she said, opening her eyes to hold his gaze, her lips curving gently as her hands grasped his shoulders.

Keeping his considerable weight off her chest, he leaned on his forearms, which were placed on either side of her, his hands near her face. Rubbing her bottom lip with his thumb, feeling the softness, he bent to kiss her as he flexed his hips, pumping in and out. She urged him on with her heels on his ass and he lost himself in her warmth.

The friction built, deep inside, and Regina felt her inner core tighten. Meeting his thrusts with her hips, she felt on the precipice, desperate for the release she knew was sure to come. Closing her eyes, she saw pinpricks of light blinking as her body coiled tighter.

"Look at me," Cael whispered, watching the play of emotions dance through her beautiful blue eyes when she opened them, her glorious hair spread over the comforter creating a shimmering halo. His cock continued to sink into her tight sex, the warmth and friction bringing him closer to his own orgasm, but he wanted her to come again first. Sliding one hand between them, he fingered her swollen clit, pinching it slightly.

Suddenly, Regina tensed as her body exploded in inner pulses that radiated throughout her being and a moan ripped from her lips.

Cael's head jerked back from the feeling, his neck straining, the muscles cording and veins prominent, as his own orgasm pulsed from his body into hers. He continued to thrust over and over until every last drop had been wrung from his body.

Barely able to think, he fell to the side, hoping he had not crushed her in the process, pulling her over so she lay sprawled on top of him.

Together, they sucked in deep breaths, their hearts racing, as their sweaty bodies slowly cooled. After a moment, she lifted her head and stared down at him. "Wow, Titan," she said, her kiss-swollen lips curved in a beautiful smile. "You got more where that came from?"

Laughing, he tightened his arms around her luscious body. "Oh, Red, we're gonna go all night."

6

Morning light peeked through the slit in the curtains, illuminating the back of Cael's eyelids. Shifting in bed a bit, before he opened his eyes he felt a warm, very female body draped over him. She was curled into his side with her leg slung over his and her arm wrapped around his middle. Her head lay on his shoulder and his arm was holding her closely to him. The feeling was unusual, considering he never spent the night with his hookups. He had been truthful with her—hookups were not frequent— but he didn't mention that he had not been in a relationship since before he had been in the Army.

He had no idea what time it was, but with the light already bright, he knew the early dawn had passed—not surprising when he considered they had spent the night burning through the strip of condoms he brought. When he had recovered after the first time, she had ridden him, her long hair forming a curtain around their heads. Then they went at each other again as they took a long shower, both discovering shower sex. The desk had not been broken in yet, but after sleeping for a while, they had woken up for another round in bed. Granted, the last time had not been particularly athletic. Instead, they had both moved slowly, discovering each other's bodies in a way that made him uncertain he wanted an early goodbye today.

Shifting slightly, he peered down into her face, memorizing the sprinkling of freckles across her nose, the dark lashes forming crescents on her cheeks, and the way her mouth was barely open emitting a cute, little snore. Blinking, he wondered what he was doing. *Why the hell am I memorizing anything about her face?* He tried to convince himself that they could walk away in the morning's light and that be it, but he knew that was not what he really wanted. *Please let her want to stay longer as well. I want more time with her...no, I need more time with her.*

As though she could hear his thoughts, her eyes opened, confusion quickly morphing into a beaming smile. " 'Morning," she said.

"Good morning to you, beautiful," he greeted. Leaning forward he kissed her gently, nipping her bottom lip.

She sat up, dragging the sheet over her breasts as she stretched. Looking down at him over her shoulder, she sighed. "I guess I'd better get dressed. I want to thank you for last night...it was way more than I ever expected. I'll just—umph," she grunted, wide-eyed, as he flipped her over onto her back, his large body pressing into hers. "What...?"

He kissed her, his tongue delving, unable to get enough of her taste. Pulling back, he held her eyes, declaring, "We need to eat."

"Eat?"

"Yeah. Breakfast."

"Breakfast?"

Chuckling, he said, "Red. Are you just gonna repeat what I say?"

Narrowing her eyes, she said, "What about our agreement?"

"We didn't say anything about not eating."

Regina bucked her hips but did not move Titan an inch. Instead, she just felt his morning wood pressed between her thighs. Eyes jerking open wide, she said, "Again? You're ready again?"

"Sorry, babe," Cael laughed. "Some things I can't control. But, I promise, no more...for now. Not until we get some fuel in us." Seeing the confusion pass through her eyes, he sobered. "Look, Red, I know we started as a hookup with no names and no regrets. But, like I said last night, one taste of you and I knew I wanted a whole night, not just an hour or two. I haven't had a whole night with someone in a very long time." He brought his hands to either side of her face, gently rubbing his thumbs over her petal soft cheeks. "Something's happening between us. I don't really know what it is, but I just know I want more time with you. I got nowhere I need to be this weekend and no one who's expecting me. I propose the whole weekend."

Sucking in her lips, Regina's chest rose and fell with

each breath, uncertainty filling her. *He wants more? More time? The whole weekend?*

"You got somewhere you need to be right now?" Cael asked, a sliver of worry now curling through him at her expression, wondering if she did not feel what he was feeling.

"No, not really. Well, actually, not at all." Her eyes sought his. "I just don't want this to get complicated."

"Won't be complicated if we keep it simple."

"Still no names and no regrets?" she asked.

"Absolutely, Red," he grinned, kissing her quickly before rolling off her. "Do you want to grab some breakfast downstairs?"

"You don't want to order room service?" she asked, wondering about wearing clothes that had been lying on the floor all night.

Jerking the sheet off her, he leered at her naked body as he jumped up from the bed. Giving her a little slap on the ass, he said, "Come on. Get dressed. We'll be spending enough of our time in this room, we might as well get out for a little while this morning."

"You are too damn cheery this early in the morning," she grumbled, climbing out of bed and grabbing her clothes from the floor. Putting them on, she looked up as he strolled from the bathroom, his jeans on, but his chest gloriously on display. "If we're going to spend the weekend together, I've got to get a toothbrush and some deodorant. Plus moisturizer."

"They got those downstairs…we can get them from housekeeping."

Cocking her hip, she glared. "And I at least need to

get some clean underwear. And don't tell me that I won't need it!"

Laughing, he said, "Well, you won't, not in here. But, we won't stay in the room the whole time, so yeah, I guess you might need a change of clothes."

She met his grin with one of her own as she pulled her clothes back on.

"Don't worry about anything…it's not a problem. They got shops nearby. After breakfast, we'll take a walk and pick up some things." He pulled his shirt over his head and smoothed out the wrinkles with his hands.

She stepped up to him and stilled his movements with her hands on his. "You're fine, Titan. In fact, you're so fine, believe me, no one will notice a wrinkle."

"I was thinking the same thing about you," he confessed. Kissing her again, he linked their fingers and they headed out of the room.

Soon ensconced in a booth with steaming cups of coffee in front of them, she ordered the French Toast breakfast with scrambled eggs and bacon. She was stunned as he ordered a double stack of pancakes, four eggs, double bacon and sausage, breakfast potatoes, and a large juice.

As soon as the food was delivered, she stared in unabashed awe as he managed to put away his entire breakfast, including part of hers that she was unable to finish.

Leaning back in his seat, he patted his stomach. "You ready to do some shopping?"

"Yes," she agreed. "I need to walk after all that food."

Grabbing her hand and gently guiding her out of the

booth, he said, "Don't worry about that. We'll work that off later." Laughing as she rolled her eyes, he led her outside and they walked down the street, their hands clasped together. The sidewalks were not crowded, but she still noticed people turning to look at them.

Looking around, she said, "You must get gawked at a lot." Settling on his face and seeing his raised eyebrow, she added, "Being so tall." She waited a beat, and asked, "How tall are you?"

Pulling on her hand so she had to stop and look up at him, he bent to kiss her. Standing up again, he replied, "Six feet, seven inches."

"Holy moly! No wonder everyone is looking at us."

"Babe, they're staring because you're so fuckin' gorgeous."

Smiling at his compliment, they continued to walk and soon came to the entrance of a park.

She gave a little tug on his hand and said, "Let's walk over there. It's so nice out today, the fresh air will do us good."

Allowing Red to lead, Cael nodded and they crossed the street. The day was perfect for a walk—sunshine, blue skies, and warm temperatures. He could not remember the last time he had done something so casual as walk hand in hand with a woman with no particular destination in mind. Glancing down at her, he noticed how her hair caught the sunlight, causing the copper and gold to shine even more. Her face was split with a wide grin as her eyes took in their surroundings.

"This is so pretty," she said. "I've never been here.

Well, I suppose on the far side, closer to the campus, I might have walked some, but this park is so huge."

"How old are you?" he asked, suddenly curious.

She shot him a glare. "First of all, it's rude to ask a lady how old they are, and second, we said anonymity."

"You tellin' me your age is hardly the same as telling me your name," he argued, "and after the night we just had, don't you think that I've proven I'm not rude?"

She barked out a laugh. "Yeah, last night was definitely not rude." Cocking her head to the side, she asked, "You afraid of robbing the cradle?" Now it was his time to glare while she just smiled before replying, "I'm twenty-eight. I was born and raised in Richmond, but left to attend UVA in Charlottesville and then did my master's work here at VCU." Grinning up at him, she lifted a brow and asked, "Good enough?"

He squeezed her fingers as he grinned. "Yeah."

"Hey, turnabout's fair play," she complained. "What about you?"

"I'm twenty-nine as well. Did four years in the Army after high school. Corps of Engineers. Like working with my hands, so I continued with construction. Work for a big company, but the work is basic conversions. Warehouses into condos, that sort of thing. I prefer restoring old houses, but for now I just do that on the side." He glanced down at her, suddenly wondering about her reaction to his confession. *Did I say too much?*

She smiled brightly and said, "I think that's wonderful to get to do what your passion is. I would hate for you to feel caged in. Do you have any hobbies?"

He warmed at her words, surprised that it mattered

to him what she thought. With another squeeze, he continued, "I've got a little house I bought and have been fixing it up on the side, so I guess my job and my hobby are one and the same."

Neither spoke for a moment as their feet took them toward a small lake in the middle of the park. The water reflected the blue sky and created a picture-perfect scene. Several benches sat facing the lake and she tugged on his hand, leading him toward one. Once seated, he threw his arm across her shoulders, tucking her into his side. She laid her head on his shoulder and they sat, quiet, appearing to any outsiders, he was sure, as a couple.

After several minutes, she leaned up and twisted her head around to peer at him. Seeing his brow lift in question, she said, "Is this weird?"

His brows lowered and he repeated, "Weird?"

Nodding, she said, "Yeah...this." When he did not respond, she continued, "Us...sitting here...like a couple. Not two strangers."

"A stranger is just a friend you haven't met yet," he said, realizing he was quoting Miss Ethel.

Her eyes widened as she said, "Uh...stranger-danger? A stranger could be a serial killer waiting to do you in."

Unable to resist, he leaned forward, whispering, "I'd like to be *in* you when I do you."

Slapping his chest with her hand, she laughed as she rolled her eyes. "Oh, God, that's bad. You are so cheesy." She held his gaze as her mirth slowed, then sighed heavily.

Before she could say anything else, he said, "Look, Red, we may have started out as a hookup, but I think we both know this is anything but just that." He watched as she sucked in her lips, thoughts moving behind her eyes. Leaning in to place a sweet kiss on her lips, he said, "There's nothing wrong with two people enjoying some time together."

Her voice soft, she said, "It feels dangerous. Like I'm playing with fire."

Kissing her once more, he said, "I promise you won't get burned with me. And when I promise something, I never beak that promise."

He expected her face to soften, but instead, she widened her eyes and snorted as she laughed. "Did you just quote Tangled to me?"

Blushing, he mumbled, "Maybe."

She grabbed his face with both of her hands and pulled him in for another kiss. Angling her head, she took the kiss deep, thrusting her tongue into his mouth. He reciprocated and the kiss lasted long minutes, until they finally separated, both panting from the sensations.

"Gotta say, Titan, never had a man quote a Disney movie to me before. But with how you said it? That was the sexiest line I've ever heard."

"Fuck, girl. If I had known Disney was all it took to pick you up, I'd have made my move quicker last night."

Giggling, she settled back into his embrace as they watched the ducks on the lake for several more minutes. "You know, ducks are fascinating. They look so calm on the top of the water, but underneath, their feet are paddling like crazy."

He opened his mouth to respond, but was unable to come up with anything to say other than to burst into laughter.

Blushing, she said, "I realize that sounded so random."

"Yeah, it did, Red. But, I gotta ask, what made you think of that?"

"I just think we're a lot like the ducks. You know, we see other people and they are so calm on the outside, but we don't really know what they have going on inside. Many of them might be paddling like crazy."

He tucked a flyaway strand of her hair behind her ear, his smile still in place. "Is that you? Are you a duck?"

Laughing, she nodded. "Yeah, sometimes I think I'm just like that."

As their mirth subsided, they continued to enjoy the view of the park, the sun shining down on them. She finally sighed and said, "As nice as this is, I still need to go shopping."

"We can come back if we want," he said, standing and linking fingers with her again, as naturally as breathing. They walked out of the park and down the street in front of the hotel.

Passing a drug store, she said, "I can run in here and grab some underwear."

Not letting go of her hand, he said, "Oh, no, Red. I got a glimpse of the green satin you've got on now and I'd like to see more. There's a lingerie shop across the street."

"Seriously?" Planting her hands on her hips, she said,

"Why should I spend money on lingerie when it's just going to be stripped off and end up on the floor?"

"Don't worry," he argued, "I'll make it worth your while. Plus, I'm buying."

Coming to a sudden halt, she planted her feet. "Oh no, you're not."

"Sure I am. I'm the one who'll benefit from the show so I'll pay."

Not allowing him to tug her further, she argued, "Titan, buying a woman underwear is not casual. It's… it's…it's personal."

Figuring he should pick his battles, and not wanting to confess that what they had was quickly becoming very personal to him, he agreed reluctantly. Entering the shop, he carefully observed as she lightly fingered the silk and satin bras and panties. Moving past the sets, she grabbed a pack of bikini panties and a sleep tank top with matching shorts. As a saleswoman approached her to talk about their newer line of exercise clothing, he nodded to another clerk, handing her his card.

She added a racer-backed tank with a pair of leggings to her purchases and moved to the register, where she pulled out her credit card. Distracted by the clerk again, she never noticed that it was not her card that was charged, nor that a few extra items had been placed in her bag. As they made their way out of the shop, he carried her bag and led them across the street.

Entering the drug store next, Regina made a beeline to the toothbrushes, deodorant, and cosmetics, grabbing her favorite shower gel and moisturizer. Meeting at the end of the aisle, she noted the large, Titan-sized box of condoms in his hand. Cocking her hip, she lifted a brow. "You must be feeling lucky."

Wrapping a long arm around her waist, he snatched her closer. Bending to take her lips, he muttered, "Oh, yeah, Red. I feel like my luck has definitely changed for the better."

Laughing, they paid for the items and headed back out. Linking fingers, Cael checked his phone but there were no updates from his sister. Red noted his worried expression and squeezed his hand. "Hey, you okay?"

Hesitating, he nodded, then decided he wanted to share at least a tidbit. "I've got a relative in the hospital and was hoping to hear something today."

"Oh, my God, Titan. I'm so sorry. Listen, you can call them. I'll go on up to the room and you can talk here. Or you go on up and I'll—"

"Hey, it's okay. If there was news, they would call. So, for now, let's go up to the room. We can relax, maybe watch a movie, have some fun, order room service later on…whatever we want."

Regina studied his profile as they entered the elevator in the hotel a few minutes later. As the doors closed, she thought about how much had changed since the night before in the same elevator. How much her heart was just a little lighter having him near. Sucking in a quick breath, she pushed those thoughts from her mind. "So, what if that *whatever* includes opening your new box of condoms?"

"Damn, Red. You are a woman after my own heart," he laughed, right before he reclaimed her lips.

7

"That's it, babe. Bring it home." Cael's hips surged upward as Red straddled him with her hands balanced on his shoulders, her mane of lion's hair hanging in a thick curtain around them and her breasts bouncing with each movement. She rocked up and down on his shaft, a sheen of perspiration on her face and chest. He swore he had never seen anyone so beautiful in his life. Right now, no other woman existed. He could not even remember the names or faces of anyone before her. His hands fondled her breasts as his fingers tugged on her nipples, eliciting more groans from her.

He felt her tiring and lifted her body slightly with his large hands to help her out. With his knees bent at the back of her, he took over the thrusting, pistoning into her warm, slick channel. Sliding his thumb to their connection, he tweaked her clit and grinned as she threw her head back, crying out as her orgasm slammed into her. He felt her inner muscles contracting on his cock and with his own roar, felt his release pour into her.

Regina felt her arms give out and flopped down on Titan's chest, utterly spent. After a moment of his hands smoothing along her back from her neck to her ass, she muttered, "Sorry."

"What the hell are you sorry for?"

"I'm squishing you but don't have the energy to roll off." She started to shift, but his hands stopped her.

"You weigh next to nothing so you're hardly squishing me. And, honest to God, if you move your body off me, I'll tan your ass."

Lifting her head, she glared into his twinkling eyes. "That's the second time you've threatened to spank me."

His hand soothed over the ass in question and he grinned. "Sound like something you'd like?"

Her nose scrunched and she admitted, "I don't know. Maybe sometime…with someone I trusted." As the words left her mouth, she realized that sometime would not include him—they only had one more day in the weekend and then reality would set in and they would part their ways…as strangers. *No names…no regrets.* Sighing, she lay her head back down on his chest.

They lay still and quiet for several minutes until he gave her a squeeze. "Let's shower and go down for dinner. Biggest meal we can come up with."

Lifting her head again, she said, "Titan, this weekend is getting expensive. Two nights at this hotel. Meals…drinks—"

"Don't worry about it. I work hard and don't play hard. That means I save most of what I earn. It's about time I spent it on something good for me." He tucked her hair behind her ear and softened his voice. "Let me do this for you."

She stared into his face, getting the feeling that this big, strong, man needed to regain some control over part of his life and this weekend was him doing just that. Nodding, she smiled. "Okay. Shower. Food. Then old movies on TV."

With a whoop, he rolled out of bed with her in his arms and headed into the bathroom.

After shower sex, as she was getting dressed, she found some sexy underwear in her bag she hadn't purchased. Rifling through the bag some more, she found the receipt and scanned it, noticing that it wasn't her card listed as the method of payment. Figuring out immediately what must have happened, she turned to Titan. "You sneak! How'd you manage this?"

Shrugging, he watched as she slipped on the blue satin panties and matching demi bra, his smile wide and gaze appreciative. "Just though you should have something nice for putting up with me all weekend."

"I should be angry, you know," she muttered, but had to admit the set was beautiful.

"Nah, life's too short to be wasted on being angry," he said, walking over to nuzzle her hair. "And seeing you, right now…you are so fuckin' worth spoiling."

Walking down the hall to the elevator, she had to admit he was right. *Life's too short to waste.*

That morning, when they had eaten breakfast, she had not looked around at the interior of the restaurant. But now, with the lights low and candles lit on each table, she noticed that the staff had arranged the tables in such a way that, while they were able to handle a crowd, they were also able to provide a quiet, private atmosphere for the patrons. Adding to that, they had scored a corner table near the back where it was even more quiet and private. She had no idea how Titan managed to snag them the best seat in the house but, with his huge size, it was not hard to image him getting his way in most things, even without ever looking askance at anyone.

"What are you thinking?"

His question cut into her musings and she blushed. "Sorry. I was just thinking that this place is really nice. I didn't notice it much this morning."

"We were hungry this morning, after last night's activities," he grinned. "It's hard to notice much when you're shoveling in fuel."

Cael watched as Red threw her head back in laughter, her hair in waves flowing down her back, long slender neck exposed. Staring at her, he could not remember the last time he had been so entranced by a woman. He thought on that for about two point five seconds before he knew the answer—*never*. What had started out as a sexual attraction was rapidly morphing into something so much more profound. He waited, wondering if a feeling of panic was finally going to descend...the desire to say goodbye and run back to his life. But all that moved through him was peace…and the desire to get to know her better.

"Tell me something about yourself," he asked, his voice low.

Her gaze jumped to his and she cocked her head to the side. "Something…personal?"

Nodding slowly, his lips curved slightly. "I want to know more about you and," he lifted his hand to cut off her protestations before she could make them, "yeah, I get that I'm changing the rules. But, then, we've already been changing the rules."

Regina looked down, her eyes following her finger moving over the rim of her wine glass. Her instinct was to refuse…to stick to the rules. Closing her eyes for an instant, she was so tired of following rules. So tired of not being in control of her life, her fate. Swallowing deeply, she lifted her gaze, her smile tremulous. She peered at his face. Hard, as if it were carved in stone, but not cold, just structured. So masculine, and yet, there was something else. A vulnerability. A glimpse of an uncertain young boy, asking but being afraid of being turned away. Her hand left her wine glass and slid across the table, resting on his.

He flipped his hand up, allowing her hand to rest in his palm. Curling his fingers around hers, he gave it a squeeze before linking fingers with her.

"My favorite color is purple. I know that seems so typically girlie, but deep purple is such a calming color. I even convinced my parents to paint my room purple… well, a light purple, but it was still the best room ever.

Even now, I have purple accents in my decorating." Her smile met his and she cocked her brow.

"Okay, okay," he agreed, "my turn." He thought for a moment, then said, "I had a teddy bear when I was a kid…not just a two-year-old kid, but I kept it until I was definitely not a kid anymore."

Her eyes warmed at this confession and her heart melted at the thought of the little boy, and not so little boy, with the teddy bear.

The server brought their appetizers and they let go of their hands to eat. Taking a bite of Thai shrimp, he chewed, swallowed, then said, "More."

Licking her lips, catching every bit of the crab dip, she cut her eyes to the ceiling in thought. "Um…when I was in tenth grade, a snooty girl at our school stole my boyfriend, so my best friend put itching powder in her cheerleading outfit…and got someone to put it in his football pants."

Barking out a laugh, he said, "Jesus, Red, remind me to never piss you off."

She laughed and defended, "Hey, I didn't do it…my friend did. Although, it was my idea."

He chuckled, shaking his head before settling his gaze back on her. "Can't imagine any man choosing someone over you."

"He was just a boy," she shrugged.

"That explains it. Most boys are dumbasses. It's only by the grace of God and a good woman that we get our heads outta our asses."

Now it was her time to laugh. The server interrupted, bringing their dinner plates. A large steak for him and the seafood platter for her. Looking at the huge servings, her eyes grew wide. "Good grief, this is a lot of food."

"Eat only what you want, babe, and I'll finish whatever you can't."

She smiled, knowing he was telling her to be comfortable and not worry about trying to eat too much. She liked that...being comfortable with him. Looking down, her heart pinged at how easy it would be to let go and let him in.

They ate in silence for several minutes, the food delicious and company easy. Spearing a luscious piece of meat, he held it over the table toward her. Leaning forward, she closed her lips around his fork, the tender morsel sliding into her mouth. Chewing, she moaned at the delectable bite and, as she lifted her eyes to him, saw the dark, intense stare he had toward her lips. The sexual tension crackled between them and she knew to other patrons they looked like a couple...a real couple.

Clearing her throat, she said, "It's your turn. Favorite music."

Blinking, Cael brought his attention from her mouth to her eyes, a slow grin spreading, knowing Red was trying to bring them back to safer ground. "That's easy. I like country. I remember my granddaddy listening to Cash and my dad listening to Nelson. I tend to go for the more recent musicians, but like the classic country as well."

"Why country?"

He thought for a moment then said, "I once heard Kenny Rogers say that the great thing about country music is it tells a story. Listen to the words and you know he's right. Each song is a story. Friendship, girls and boys, love, hurt, fun, heartache…it's all there."

"Wow," she said, "I like country music also but never thought about it in those terms. You're right."

He had finished his steak and she pushed her plate over to him, giving him permission to finish the last of her shrimp and scallops. "You?"

Taking a final sip of her wine, she shook her head. "I'm all over the place with music. When I'm in the car, I love listening to country. But, at work, I listen to new age instrumental." A giggle slipped out as she admitted, "And, from Thanksgiving through Christmas, I listen to holiday music non-stop."

Deciding to split a dessert, they dove into the crème brulee, play-battling with their spoons.

"So, when did you get the growth spurt, Mr. Humongous?"

He shot her a pretend glare before answering. "I probably hit my first growth spurt when I was about twelve. By the time I was fourteen, I was six feet tall. By the time I was sixteen, I was six feet five inches. I finally stopped at six feet seven."

"Holy moly," she exclaimed, eyes wide. "They must have wanted you for basketball!"

Nodding he said, "Yeah, but I hated the game. Don't mind watching it but didn't want to play it. I was into baseball."

"Power hitter," she claimed.

"The basketball coach in high school tried to bully

me into playing, but Miss Ethel told me to stick to my guns and do what felt right."

"Miss Ethel?"

Leaving the last bite for her, he replied, "My foster mom." As soon as the words left his mouth, he jerked his gaze up to hers.

She stared for a millisecond before smiling slowly. "It's okay, Titan. I know we said no names, but I like that we're sharing."

"I didn't mean to share something so personal," he admitted. "You're just easy to talk to."

"I was thinking the same thing about you."

The server brought the check and, without taking his eyes from Red, he gave the room number to charge the meal to his card on hold.

Reaching his hand out as he stood, he gently assisted her from her chair. Wrapping his arm around her shoulders, he moved them through the room and toward the elevator. Time for talking was over.

8

Cael braced his weight on his forearms, each of his large hands on either side of Red's face, his calloused thumbs soothing her cheeks. His hips moved in rhythm, sliding his cock in and out of her warm sex. Her legs were wrapped around his waist, her heels pressing on his ass. Her hair flowed out across the pillow, creating a halo.

Staring into his eyes, neither speaking, she focused on the movement and friction, not on the emotions sliding through her. This was supposed to be simply sex...fun...casual. But the intense look in his eyes as his body moved in hers, was so much more than casual. As her core wound tighter, she emptied her mind of everything but the physical sensations, allowing her orgasm to take her to heights she had never experienced before. Her fingers dug into his shoulders as she cried out her body's response.

Watching her face, as she gave herself to him, struck Cael as the most beautiful thing he had ever witnessed. Her channel tightened and he resisted the desire to thrust harder and faster, instead forcing himself to prolong the intensity. As she slowly relaxed and her eyes drifted open once more, he planted himself deep inside, his muscles tensing, his orgasm flooding from his body into hers. Dropping his head to the side of hers, he sucked in raspy breaths until his heartbeat slowed. Lifting his head again, he peered down at her, seeing a lazy smile on her face. Meeting her grin, he rolled off, pulling her close.

"No way."

"Yes, I'm telling you that's why she only did two movies for him." Red popped another piece of popcorn in her mouth.

"But—" Cael began.

"Serious, Titan, I know what I'm talking about. Hitchcock always had a thing for his leading ladies and when Tippi Hedren did The Birds, he creeped her out. Part of her contract was to go around and promote the movie with him and he put the moves on her."

He shifted his eyes from the TV screen where the big, black birds were perched on the playground equipment and watched her grinning at him. A dollop of butter was on the corner of her mouth and her tongue darted out to lick it off. His heart pinged, but he pushed that thought away. Leaning forward, he grinned, "Let me get that." Kissing her mouth, his tongue darted out, tasting the salty butter. Smacking his lips, he sat back and said, "So, Tippi and Alfred?"

"Well, he wanted her to do more movies for him but she only did one more. It was Marnie with Sean Connery."

Cocking his head, he said, "I thought I knew all of Hitchcock's movie, but that one doesn't ring a bell."

"I, personally, didn't like it. It was creepy, like most of his, and Sean played a real dick. But anyway, afterwards, Tippi refused to do any more movies for Hitchcock."

"Okay, what's your favorite Hitchcock movie?"

An embarrassed grin slid over her face, and she said, "Well, it's not my absolute favorite, but he did one that was really different. It was more of a mystery comedy titled Family Plot. William Devane, Karen Black, Barbara Harris, and Bruce Dern."

Laughing, he said, "Oh, my God, I forgot Hitchcock directed that."

"It was his last film."

She pushed the empty popcorn bowl away and said, "God, I'm stuffed." Curling up to his side, they lay entwined, reclining on the bed.

"What other movies do you like?" he asked, with his head propped up on one hand and the other hand trailing paths over her hips.

"I love old movies. Like really, really old movies." Looking at him hesitantly, she added, "I actually studied them in school."

Wide eyed, he said, "Seriously?"

"Well, I do restoration on old films. I turned a love of old films into a career." They were quiet for a moment, as she worked up her courage and asked, "Can you tell me about your house? The one you're working on?"

His eyes held hers and the air changed between them...something tangible, taking them further from their bubble of anonymity.

"Bought it for a song when I got out of the service. There was nothing wrong with it...just old. The former owners had had it for years and decided to move to a retirement community so they were ready to sell. The bones of the house were solid, it just needed to be brought into this century."

He watched as she smiled, glad that she was interested, and continued, "I had to deal with the bathrooms and kitchen, refinished the hardwood floors and put in new windows. With paint, indoors and out, it's been a nice house to own."

"Are you all finished with working on it?"

Barking out laugh, he said, "Nah. It's pretty small, so I'm adding an addition to the back. It'll have a large den and laundry room on the first floor and a master suite on the second floor."

"Wow, I'm so impressed," Regina said, enjoying Titan's animated expressions as he talked with such affection about his home.

Shrugging, he said, "I get to do what I love, not only in my job but making my home fit me."

She nodded, but remained quiet, a soft smile curving her lips.

Cael wrapped his arm around Red, pulling her close as their Hitchcock marathon continued. She felt good in his arms, her head resting on his chest and her hand gently laying on his abs. There was something so strong, and yet so fragile about her. His fingers slid through her hair, the play of light on the various colors of red and blonde holding his attention.

Everything about her captured his attention. She was funny, smart, and so beautiful. But tomorrow he was back to work and, hopefully, back to visiting his niece soon. *No names and no regrets.* So why was he already feeling them?

Standing in the lobby the next morning, Regina forced a smile as she peered up at Titan. Placing her hand on his wide chest, her fingertips were now used to the play of muscles under his shirt. Something had happened that morning in the early light. When he woke, instead of wild sex, he had moved over her body reverently. Their movements had been slow…deliberate… almost…*making love.* Soft kisses. Gentle touches. Regret snaked through her but she pushed it back.

"This has been an amazing weekend—" she began.

"I want more," he announced suddenly, his intense stare holding her in place. Seeing her hesitation, he said, "This. Whatever this is…I don't want it to end here."

She continued to stare at him, uncertainty filling her soul. Still, desperate to see him again, she waited to see what he proposed.

"I have work during the day, but my nights are free. At least for now. My friend in the hospital can't have visitors for a few more days."

"Won't this just make it harder to say goodbye later?"

"I don't care about later. I just want more of now."

His face, already so familiar to her, was filled with longing. She had no idea what *this* was. They still had not shared names. *Even friends with benefits know each other's names.* Her heart beat faster as she acknowledged she wanted to see him again. *With everything going on in my life...I just want something that I can hold on to when things get rough. Even if it's just memories and regrets.* Nodding slowly, she agreed silently, then smiled as relief flooded his eyes.

Bending, he kissed her lips and said, "I get off work at about four o'clock. I'll meet you here in the lobby at five. Is that okay?"

"Okay. Here, tonight at five." Lifting on her toes, she wrapped her arms around his neck and pressed her lips against his. "See you later, Titan." With a wink, she turned and walked through the glass door and into the waiting taxi.

Cael stood, solid, for a moment, hands on his hips, watching as she walked away. "Bye, Red," he whispered, hoping she would appear that night.

The day dragged on and by four o'clock Cael was antsy. As he drove home to shower and change, he called his sister, hating to hear the fatigue in her voice. "Are they still keeping other visitors out?"

"Yeah. It's not been a good day. She began throwing up and has felt horrible all day. She keeps asking for you and can't understand why the hospital won't let you come."

"Shit, sis. She probably thinks I don't want to be there—"

"No, no, Cael, I explained to her that you really wanted to be here but they wouldn't let you."

They were silent for a few seconds and he became uneasy. "Sis, what aren't you telling me?" He heard a quick intake of breath, before she replied, her voice quivering.

"Her hair started falling out over the weekend. So much faster than we thought it would. I was brushing and a lot came out…some in clumps."

"Fuckin' hell!" he cursed, feeling helpless, not an emotion he liked at all. "What can I do?"

"I don't know. Nothing I suppose. Wait…yes. Can you buy a scarf or something like that? When you come we can tie it around her head. She sees other kids here with those and said she would like one too."

"No problem. I'll have it for when they finally let me visit. Tell her I love her, and sis…take care of yourself too." Disconnecting, he pulled into his driveway, his heart aching. The thought slid through his mind that perhaps he should stay home. *What the hell am I doing with Red anyway? It can't go anywhere.* Climbing the stairs to his small house, his steps were as heavy as his heart.

Regina sat in the lobby on a red leather sofa, her eyes trained on the front door. Wiping her hands on her clean jeans, she looked down, straightening her blue blouse. She had considered not coming, but she had said she would and did not want to break a promise. *What am I doing? Could the timing possibly be worse?*

Blowing out a breath, she puffed her hair from her face, before sliding her hand over the long tresses, smoothing them down. Several men walked by, appreciation on their faces, but she ignored them. There was only one man she was interested in and she kept watch, hoping to see him coming through the front door. With no sight of him, she looked down at her clasped hands.

Suddenly, the sound of heavy boots on the floor reverberated through her and she did not have to look up to know who was making that sound. A smile curved her lips as she finally lifted her head to see his massive body, clad in jeans and a dark green polo, stalking toward her. He was the hunter and she, the prey. She had never desired to be caught before but, now? All she wanted was for this man to claim her.

Standing as he approached, he moved directly into her space, his arms enveloping her into his embrace as he bent to kiss her lips. She clung to him, unheeding of any passersby in the lobby.

As they separated, he grinned down at her. "Glad you're here, Red."

Laughing, she replied, "Back at you, Titan."

Slinging his arm over her shoulder, he said, "I'm in the mood for a big, juicy burger." Leering down, he added, "For starters."

Arm in arm, they walked toward the hotel's restaurant. Once settled in an intimate, corner booth, their orders given, he admitted, "I have to confess, the idea of not coming ran through my mind. I feel like I should apologize for that."

Holding his sincere gaze, she said, "I understand. What we're doing doesn't make any sense. I wondered if I should come as well. But, once I got here, I really wanted you to show up."

They reached out, at the same time, fingers linking together on the middle of the table. "I have no idea what we're doing, but I wasn't ready to give it up yet," she said.

The candlelight sent shimmers through Red's hair, capturing Cael's attention. The similarity between her hair and his niece's shorn tresses caused his breath to catch in his throat. Blinking, he said, "Let's enjoy our time."

Two hours later, she was settled between his thighs, her head back against his shoulder, as the hot water in the garden tub rose closer to the top. The room was lit with scented candles and they both sighed in relaxation.

"Tell me more about the man who can quote Gulliver's Travels," she asked, her hands moving in circles in the water, watching the play of the candlelight on the surface.

He was quiet for a moment, then, shared, "I had a brother who used to read to us every night. He had several abridged books of classics and fairytales. So, I grew up listening to shortened versions of famous novels and stories. After a while, quotes came naturally to me, especially when they applied to life."

"I loved fairy tales when I was growing up, too," she

said. "I loved the classics…the ones that Disney later turned into movies, but then I also loved the little-known ones as well."

They remained silent for several minutes, each to their own thoughts. Twisting her head around, she asked, "Why do you think we love fairy tales so much?"

"'Fairy tales are more than true: not because they tell us that dragons exist, but because they tell us that dragons can be beaten.'" Seeing the unspoken question in her eyes, he shook his head. "No, that's not from me, although the words are exactly what I feel. It's from a British writer, Neil Gaiman."

"His words are so true," she agreed, relaxing against his chest again. "We all want to feel that we can beat the dragons in our lives."

Taking the washcloth, Cael gently soothed it over her skin, now pink from the warm water, wondering about the dragons in her life. He opened his mouth, ready to ask…putting himself out there to tell as well. Hesitating, he was about to speak, when she twisted completely in the water and straddled his hips. His cock, already at attention, jumped at the contact of her channel.

All thoughts flew out of his mind as she lifted up and asked, "Do condoms work underwater?"

"Fuck," he cursed, standing while plucking her up in his arms at the same time. Stepping sure-footed onto the bathmat, he reached over to grab one. "They might tear in the water but, damn, the sight of you about ready to sink down on me nearly had me forgetting all else."

It was on the tip of Regina's tongue to say that she

was clean and on the pill, but she stayed silent, knowing that it was not worth the risk with a man who was still a mystery to her in so many ways. Before regrets set in at that fact, he stalked to the bed, lying her on her back gently.

Pushing her hair from her face, Cael stared down at her beauty. With slow reverence, he caressed her body, discovering every sensitive spot along with every curve. When finished, long hours later, she lay languid in his arms all night.

9

Cael stepped off the elevator, walking briskly down the hall toward Cindy's room. His hand was clutched around a special scarf that he hoped she would like. He moved to the prep station, washing his hands and donning a paper gown and mask. Standing outside her door for a moment, he hesitated, swallowing deeply. Clearing the fear from his face, he knocked and entered.

The shock of seeing his niece, so different than she was mere days ago, caused his feet to stumble and he was thankful for the mask hiding half of his face. Her tiny body was buried under blankets. Dark circles underneath her eyes stood out in stark relief to her pale complexion. She had a light pink scarf tied around her head and the reality of her situation gripped his heart in a vise.

"Uncle Cael," she smiled.

"Hey, Beautiful Cindy-Loo," he called out, continuing into the room, dropping a kiss on Kathy's head before leaning down to kiss Cindy's cheek.

"Sweetie, I think Uncle Cael brought you something."

She looked from her mother to him and grinned as he lifted his hand, holding a cute, stretchy turban covered in Disney princesses. She immediately reached for it, saying, "Mommy, put it on me."

Kathy unwound the scarf, baring Cindy's tiny, bald head. Keeping hold of his niece's hand, he squeezed it in comfort, blinking at the stinging in his eyes. Kathy slipped the perfectly fitting turban over her head and handed her a mirror. Cindy squealed in delight, turning her head back and forth as she called out each princess' name.

Kathy mouthed *Thank You*, but he waved her thanks away. Tom came in and expressed delight as Cindy showed off her new headdress to her dad.

"I wasn't sure what size to get," he admitted, "so I'm glad you like it. There are others I'll get as well."

Cindy looked up at him, her smile slipping slightly. "Mommy," she turned to Kathy, "will I be bald for a long time?"

The three adults hesitated before Kathy, sitting on the bed with Cindy, kissed her and said, "I don't know, baby. But, we'll make sure you have fun hats for as long as you need them."

Satisfied with that answer, she snuggled down under the covers once more as Cael sat nearby and pulled out his book.

"I want the Velveteen Rabbit, Uncle Cael. I want to hear about how he was loved."

Nodding at Kathy and Tom who were going downstairs to the cafeteria, he reached over and placed his large hand on Cindy's tiny one, rubbing it gently as he began to read.

"There was once a velveteen rabbit, and in the beginning he was really splendid. He was fat and bunchy, as a rabbit should be; his coat was spotted brown and white, he had real thread whiskers, and his ears were lined with pink sateen. On Christmas morning, when he sat wedged in the top of the Boy's stocking, with a sprig of holly between his paws, the effect was charming."

Cindy smiled, her hand searching the bed through her various stuffed animals until coming upon the rabbit. Pulling it in close, she nodded for him to continue. As he read, he hesitated when he reached a certain part, stumbling over the words, having forgotten how the story took a sad turn.

"'Real isn't how you are made,' said the Skin Horse. 'It's a thing that happens to you. When a child loves you for a long, long time, not just to play with, but REALLY loves you, then you become Real....

"'Generally, by the time you are Real, most of your hair has been loved off...But these things don't matter at all, because once you are Real you can't be ugly, except to people who don't understand.'"

Her wide eyes stared back at him, as she asked, "Is that what happened to me? My hair was loved off?"

Wishing Kathy had returned to answer Cindy's difficult questions, he sighed heavily. "Sort of," he improvised. "Some of the medicine you take makes you lose your hair, but you take the medicine because we love you so much and want you to get better. So, in a way, because you are so loved, your hair is loved off."

She appeared to ponder his response before settling back into the bed and he wiped his sweaty palms on his jeans.

As he finished the story, he observed her eyes were closed and her breathing slow and even.

"When the Fairy kissed him that last time, she had changed him altogether...He was a Real rabbit at last, at home with the other rabbits."

Swallowing hard, tears pricked his eyes and before he was able to stop it, one fell down his cheeks landing on his chest.

Sitting on the same red leather sofa in the lobby as the night before, Regina waited, but as the minutes ticked by, her heart began to sink. Fifteen minutes after five o'clock. She wiped imaginary lint from her dark pink blouse, once more ignoring the looks from other men as they walked by. The lobby was busy as guests moved between the elevators to the reception desk to the restaurant. Twenty minutes late. The tantalizing scents from the restaurant wafted by. Twenty-five minutes late.

Dropping her chin to her chest, she vowed that at five-thirty she would leave. *It was a good run. A good time.* Sighing, she repeated silently, *no names and no regrets.* But, she knew she had failed the second one. Hearing the large clock in the lobby chime the half-hour, she stood, slinging her purse onto her shoulder. Walking briskly to the door, she moved through it and onto the street. Turning to the right, she was determined to go to the park, even if it did bring back some memories. Crossing the street, she just made it to the entrance when she heard someone shout, "Red!"

Heart pounding, she turned and saw Titan jogging toward her.

Cael knew he was running late. Kathy and Tom ended up speaking to Cindy's oncologist as they came back from their dinner. He had been glad for them to have the time but, at the same time, he had no way to contact Red. He had just turned the corner to enter the hotel lobby when he saw her crossing the street heading to the park. Taking off running, he called out her name, hoping she could hear him.

As he neared, he observed her face shining in the evening light, her lips curving into a smile as she recognized him. Stunned at the track of wet tears on her cheeks, he braced as she took off running toward him, jumping at the last second. He caught her easily and, holding her familiar body close, kissed her as she cupped his cheeks.

Regina did not know what was different, but his kiss seemed to pour his soul into her. Leaning back, she peered at him. "Are you okay?"

Nodding, he replied, "I got held up at the hospital."

"Your friend?"

"Uh…yeah." With her still in his arms, he said, "You want to get some food before we go back to the hotel?"

"Of course," she said with a smile. He started

walking and she laughed. "Do you want to put me down?"

"Nope."

Still grinning, she wiggled and he slowly set her feet onto the ground. They linked hands and walked to a little Italian restaurant down the street. Sitting at a checkered-cloth table near the front window, they sipped their wine and dined on pasta and shrimp.

At one point, she looked over and noticed him staring at her, a strange expression on his face. Tilting her head to the side, she said, "Hey, whatcha thinking?"

His hand reached out, touching her hair and he said, "Your hair was the first thing I noticed at the bar the night we met."

She smiled and explained, "My grandmother had reddish hair. My father did too, but he lost his early."

At the thought of losing hair, Cael blinked, his smile faltering. Recovering, he said, "It's beautiful."

That night at the hotel, Red lay under him, his weight resting on his muscular forearms as he moved in and out of her tight, slick sex. Slowly. Deliberately. His hands cupped her head and he rubbed his thumbs over her cheeks. Kissing her, his tongue moved in time with his hips, thrusting in long, lazy strokes.

The friction built and Regina wrapped her legs around his waist, wanting to hold him as close as possible. Her body tightened and she fell over the edge. He came soon after, both of them gasping at the emotions that rocked them. He rolled to the side, taking her with him and pulling the covers up to keep them cocooned in warmth, holding her tight as they slept.

Determined to not be late, Cael raced through traffic to get to the hotel. This was officially the last night that he and Red had planned on seeing each other, but his heart wanted more. Tonight's the night...*I'll ask her for her name.*

Walking into the lobby, he made a beeline for the red sofa, not seeing her but knowing he was the one who was early for once. Sitting, he realized how nerve-racking it was being the one waiting. Grateful when she entered, he grinned at her wide-eyed surprise. Standing to kiss her, his phone vibrated in his pocket.

Apologizing, he looked down at the screen and saw a text from his sister. **Can you come? Cindy's having a bad night and is asking for you.**

Dragging his hand through his hair, he looked into Red's face. "Jesus, babe, I'm so sorry, but I'm needed at the hospital."

Concerned, she gushed, "Of course. Absolutely, you must go."

"Come with me," he said, impulsively.

Stunned, she shook her head as she stared into his pleading eyes. "But, I...we..."

"Please, come with me."

The urgency with which he said those four words left Regina nodding before she consciously made the decision to go. Uncertain about the wisdom of her choice, she knew she wanted to be with him. He needed her, and she wanted to be there for him. Watching him visibly relax, she linked fingers with him and said, "Let's go."

He sent a quick text but they spoke very little on the way to the hospital. When they turned into the Children's Hospital, she stared, surprised. As they entered, he walked her to the reception desk to receive her visitor's badge.

Turning toward her, he confessed, "It's my niece. She's getting treatments here. I try to see her everyday but some days are better than others." As they approached the hall, he said, "We have to get scrubbed here. I'll let my sister know you're here before we go in. I'm sure she would like to meet you."

"No, I can just stay here—"

"I'd like you with me." Cael squeezed Red's hand, hoping she could feel how much he needed her. Smiling as she nodded again, he led her to the prep station. He showed her the routine and she completed it along with him. Donning a gown and mask, they walked down the hall.

At the door, Regina hung back, grateful when he explained the procedure for needing permission first—she wanted to give him and his family privacy. He walked into the room and she shifted her stance so she could see him.

Peeking through the window, his massive back was all she could see until he circled the bed and her eyes landed on a tiny, sweet-faced little girl. She was clad in a pink gown with several stuffed animals sharing the bed with her. Her pale face beamed as she peered up at her uncle. *Her uncle. Jesus, I don't even know his name.*

Blowing out a breath, she observed the child's head was covered in a stretchy turban decorated with Disney princesses. Sucking in a shuddering breath, she wondered what she was doing here.

As he bent to hug his niece, her heart melted. She might not know his name, but she knew him. And liked what she knew.

A woman appeared in the doorway, her face tired, but she smiled. "Hey, I'm Kathy…Cindy's mom."

Startled, she jumped. "Oh, I'm just a friend of…of—"

Kathy laughed and said, "It's okay. He sent a text saying he was bringing a special friend and I wasn't allowed to ask questions." She cocked her head to the side and asked, "Would you like to come in?"

Hesitating, she said, "Oh, I don't think so. I wouldn't want to upset your daughter—"

"Don't worry about it. Her room is a constant revolving door of people coming and going…most wanting to poke or prod her. She'd love to see someone new."

Following Kathy into the room, she entered slowly, making her way to the side where Titan was sitting, holding Cindy's hand. The little girl's eyes instantly shot up to her, widening.

"Oh, you're so pretty. You look like a princess," Cindy said, her voice weak.

Cael turned and smiled over his shoulder at Red before standing. "Cindy, this is my friend. I call her Red because of her hair."

Cindy's eyes stayed wide as they traveled down the length of her hair. "My hair used to be just like that," she said, "Same color and everything, but it had to all go away. Mom says it'll grow back and be prettier than ever."

"I'm sure it will, Cindy," she said. Before she had a chance to say anything else, Cindy turned to him and confessed, "I was throwing up earlier. I wanted you to read me a story."

"You got it, Cindy-Loo." He settled into the chair again and motioned for Red to take a seat as well, but she declined.

"Go ahead. I'll just stand back here." Regina moved toward the door and leaned against the wall.

Kathy joined her and said, "If you're okay here with them, I'm going to run to the parents' lounge and take a quick shower."

"Of course," she assured, her heart aching for the young mother who had to sneak out to get something as simple as a shower. She watched as Kathy grabbed a small overnight bag and headed out the door.

"I want her to sit with me," Cindy said, speaking to her uncle but with her eyes fixed on her.

He twisted around, his gaze imploring. Smiling, she walked forward and sat on the side of Cindy's bed, taking the little girl's hand in hers. Nodding toward him, she watched as he held his niece's other hand while reading from a book, open in his lap.

"Rapunzel had magnificent long hair, fine as spun gold, and when she heard the voice of the enchantress she unfastened her braided tresses, wound them round one of the hooks of the window

above, and then the hair fell twenty ells down, and the enchantress climbed up by it."

"What's an ell?" Cindy asked, interrupting the story.

Cael grinned because she always asked the same question when he read Grimm's version of Rapunzel. "I think it's probably a foot. So, I guess her hair was over twenty feet long." Continuing the story, he watched her settle again.

"But the king's son began to talk to her quite like a friend, and told her that his heart had been so stirred that it had let him have no rest, and he had been forced to see her. Then Rapunzel lost her fear, and when he asked her if she would take him for her husband, and she saw that he was young and handsome, she thought, he will love me more than the old witch does. And she said yes, and laid her hand in his."

At these words, he looked up at Red, his heart in his throat. Tight emotion coiled inside, warring with his head. She stared at him with wide-eyes, the rest of her face hidden behind the hospital mask.

"Keep going," Cindy demanded, her face turned toward him.

He continued the story, but stumbled over the passage about Rapunzel's hair.

"In her anger she clutched Rapunzel's beautiful tresses, wrapped them twice round her left hand, seized a pair of scissors with the right, and snip, snap, they were cut off, and the lovely braids lay on the ground. And she was so pitiless that she took poor

Rapunzel into a desert where she had to live in great grief and misery."

"I felt sad when Mommy cut my hair," Cindy confessed, clutching her bear tightly.

"Oh, baby, I'm so sorry," he said, his voice cracking, his hand instinctively squeezing her tiny one.

She sighed, the blanket barely moving with the exertion. "You promised it would grow back."

"I still promise that, sweetheart. One day, you will look in the mirror and see that your beautiful face will have beautiful hair framing it. And until then, you will always see your beautiful face."

Still sitting on the bed, Regina grabbed the frame, afraid if she did not, she would collapse backward. Pressing her fingers to her mouth to still the sob wanting to escape, she blinked in a furious attempt to quell the tears forming. She forced herself to listen as Titan finished the story.

"The prince heard a voice, and it seemed so familiar to him that he went towards it, and when he approached, Rapunzel knew him and fell on his neck and wept. Two of her tears wetted his eyes and they grew clear again, and he could see with them as before. He led her to his kingdom where he was joyfully received, and they lived for a long time afterwards, happy and contented."

"Will I meet a handsome prince?" Cindy asked, a yawn following her question and her eyes barely open.

Cael bent over her body and kissed her forehead through his mask. "All princesses meet their princes and you are no different. Someday a prince, worthy of you, will come."

She twisted around to look at Red before sliding her eyes back to him. "Are you her handsome prince?"

He opened and closed his mouth several times without speaking. "I'm…uh…not sure."

Cindy looked back at Red, her nose scrunched and asked, "Will you come back and see me sometime?"

Without thinking, Regina nodded. "Yeah, baby. I'll be with you."

With that, they watched as she fell asleep.

Standing, Cael watched as Red stood as well and moved to the door, her eyes full of tears. Placing her hand on the frame, she turned back to him, locking eyes with his and exposing all the sorrow she felt. Emotions flooded him. Desire to comfort her warring with the responsibility he felt towards his niece. She needed his full attention right now, there wasn't room in his life for anything else. Swallowing with difficulty, he walked toward Red but Kathy entered before he had a chance to say anything. As he said goodbye to his sister, Red slipped out of the door.

He found her a few minutes later in the waiting room by the elevators, her gown and mask removed. Her eyes were now dry, the mascara trails wiped clean.

Catching sight of him, Regina offered a gentle smile as she moved to him, wrapping her arms around his middle. She looked up into his face, but his expression was unreadable. Keeping quiet, she waited to see what he needed.

"Ready?" he said softly.

She wondered if he meant ready to leave the hospital and go their separate ways, or ready for more of them. Deciding either was fine with her, she just nodded. Once on the road, he kept his fingers linked with hers and she observed the city's lights as they made their way back to the hotel, feeling in the air that something between them had changed.

10

Once in the room, he took his time, slowly undressing her. Peeling her blouse from her shoulders, he kissed her neck as his hands caressed each inch of her. Her light blue, satin bra fell to the floor and he bent to carefully unfasten her pants, pulling them down along with her satin panties. Completely naked, Regina stood before him, feeling strangely exposed to this man who had come to know her body intimately.

Standing, his gaze skimmed her body from her painted toenails, traveling up her long legs, to her breasts, and landing on her face. He reached up, smoothing her hair back from her forehead, then, slid his hands down the long, silky tresses glistening in the soft lights of the room.

"So fucking beautiful, Red," he said and she smiled softly. "You know, you never call me Titan anymore. In fact, now that I think about it, you haven't said that for several days."

She lifted her hands and placed them on his shoulders, feeling the tension in his thick muscles. Shaking her head, she replied, "It was a silly name...one that was easy to use between strangers." Lifting her shoulders in a light shrug, she added, "You're no longer a stranger."

Cael's breath caught in his throat for a second before he bent to take Red's lips in a barely-there kiss. Reverently tasting her, memorizing her. He led her to the bed before he began to peel off his clothes. She watched eagerly as he removed his shirt, exposing the play of muscles that corded with each of his movements. As he stepped out of his pants and boxers and reached for the nightstand to grab a condom, she halted his hands.

Kneeling on the floor at his feet, Regina gently encircled his cock with her hands, the satin and steel shaft familiar. Slipping her lips over the tip, she slid him into her mouth, gliding her tongue along the length.

Cael hissed through his teeth at the sensation of her warm mouth enveloping, him almost causing him to come immediately. He stared down at her head, her face hidden behind the curtain of her golden-red hair. In danger of falling to the floor to worship her, he forced his legs to lock in place, threading his hands in her tresses.

As she pumped the base with her hand, she moved her mouth up and down, eliciting moans from both of them. When he could tell he was about to come, he tried to pull away. She held tight to his ass with her other hand and before he could attempt to control himself, his orgasm blasted into her mouth. Without hesitation she continued to suck, swallowing each drop.

Spent, he barely managed to scoop her up and deposit her onto the bed before landing next to her. "Fuck, baby. Fuck. Your mouth is as sweet as the rest of you."

Kissing him, Regina gave herself to him. Heart and soul, she gave everything she had.

They lay in each other's arms, legs entangled, after making love long into the night. His hand had caressed her shoulder as Regina closed her eyes and began to drift.

She stayed quiet, the sound of his strong heartbeat against her cheek, comforting, even though it couldn't drown out her tumultuous thoughts. *How can this go on? How can I tell him everything, when that would tear us apart? If only we'd met at another time...in another place. But, now that I have him, how can I let him go?* The quiet night gave no answers but, just as sleep was about to claim her, he gave them to her.

Cael waited until he thought Red was asleep, his mind churning at the agony of this wonderful woman entering his life now, when there was too much going on to keep her. Sure that she was deep in slumber, he whispered into the night, "I wanted this to be fun. One night, no names and no regrets. Then, I wanted it to last, for a little while longer. But now, sweet Red, I've got no place in my life for more than what is already there. I've got to give everything to my family. There's nothing left to give."

He sighed, his breath leaving his lungs in a sad exhalation, feeling as though his heart could take no more. Closing his eyes, he allowed his thoughts to ease as sleep finally claimed him.

In his arms, absorbing all that he had said, a silent tear slid down her face.

An hour later, she slipped from his arms and silently dressed. Writing a note on the hotel paper, she left it by his wallet on the table. Tiptoeing back to the edge of the bed, she stared down at him, his handsome face relaxed in slumber. She reached her hand out, itching to caress his stubbled jaw once more, but she halted an inch from his cheek. Bringing her hand back, she pressed her fingers to her lips. Swallowing a tear, she turned and silently walked out the door.

Cael's dreams were filled with visions of people in his life swirling, as though in a fog. His father, mother, sister, Miss Ethel, Zander, Rafe, Asher, Jayden, Jaxon, Zeke, and the others who moved in and out of his life. He saw himself as a scared child, sitting on his new bed, Miss Ethel sitting with him as she tucked him in. *"Cael, remember that nothing is as important as family. Of course, family is not just those we are born into, but the families that we make as well."* Red's beautiful face came into his dream next, pale and delicate. *She can be my family too.* He reached toward her but her image faded into the fog.

He stirred, the first dawning of light peeking into

the room. Stretching, his body was relaxed after a deep sleep and from the lovemaking the night before. Suddenly aware of the empty bed beside him, he jerked his head to the side to confirm Red was not there. Listening for sounds from the bathroom, it was eerily quiet. Sitting up, his eyes landed on the floor where her clothes had been dropped the night before. Now, the floor only contained his clothes. Jumping up, he hurried to the bathroom to check, but it was empty.

Rushing to get dressed, determined to head to the restaurant to see if she had gone down for breakfast, he spied a piece of folded paper on the table. With shaking hands, he snatched it up, unfolding it, his eyes devouring the words.

Thank you so much for the past week. It has been the most memorable week of my life. And thank you for sharing a bit of your family with me last night. It was an honor to meet them. I know we said no names and no regrets. We held to the first, but I am in danger of ruining the second. Spending more time with you would only lead to them, so I am slipping out, trying to be strong, because a goodbye would be too difficult. I pray your sweet niece gets better soon and that you find the happily-ever-after you seek.

Your Red

His heart ached as his knees gave out, causing him to stumble backward into the chair. He thought back to the dream he just awoke from, Miss Ethel's words coming hours too late for him to share with Red. He had no idea how long he stayed in the chair before he finally rose, finished dressing, and walked to the door of room 917. Staring for a moment at the bed, now as familiar as the one in his house, the covers were messy from their lovemaking and sleep. Sucking in a deep breath, he turned and walked out the door, closing it with a resounding click behind him.

Turning in his room card at the reception desk, he grimaced when the receptionist asked if his stay had been a good one. Nodding, he managed to say, "Yeah. It was great."

"And will you be needing the room for another night?"

Shaking his head, he choked out, "No. I'm all done here." Walking through the lobby, peaceful in the early morning, he glanced at the red sofa where she had perched each day waiting for him. As he headed through the main doors, he inhaled the cool air and made his way to his truck. Alone.

Cael's zombie performance the next day at work had Terrance sending him home early. "You're a danger to yourself and your crew. Go home. Rest. Go see your niece. But get some fuckin' sleep, man."

Irritated with himself, he drove, still on autopilot, to the hospital. Scrubbed and masked, he entered Cindy's room, seeing her sleeping, with Kathy and her mother-in-law each reading in a chair nearby.

Kathy looked up and smiled, then lifted her hand to indicate for him to stop while she rose from her seat. Moving toward him, she said, "She's been sleeping. With her grandmother here, let's get a cup of coffee."

Nodding his thanks to Tom's mother, he walked out of the room with Kathy in tow and they headed to the coffee shop at the corner of the hospital's cafeteria. After placing their order, they moved to a small table by a sunny window.

"So, tell me about your lady friend," she began.

Fiddling with his napkin, he shrugged. "Nothing to tell. Met her in a bar…we had some laughs, some good times. But, it's time to move on." He kept his eyes down, not wanting her to see the emotion in his eyes.

Silence moved between them and he gratefully looked at the server as their coffee was delivered along with two savory muffins.

"Cael…look at me."

Raising his eyes, his brow crinkled. "Seriously, sis? You sound like you're talking as a parent to a child right now." She laughed out loud, her eyes twinkling and he realized it had been a long time since he had seen that look on her face. Shaking his head, he said, "God, I'm sorry. About a lot of things."

She reached out and placed her hand on his arm, saying, "Tell me." At his hesitation, she quickly added, "Please. I'm so tired of being in my head, trying to handle everything that needs to be dealt with for Cindy. My world has narrowed to chemo meds, nausea meds, port lines, fluids, and a million medical words I don't know. I'd kill for a chance to be useful somewhere else and to listen to someone else for a change. Please, Cael, indulge me. Talk to me."

He stared for a moment, realizing that, for Kathy, her world had changed drastically over the last few months. Blowing out a long breath, he said, "The first part of what I said was true. We met in a bar. It was her hair that caught my attention. It looked so much like dad's...remember?" She nodded, and he continued, "I'd been drinking and hoped for an easy pick-up, but we started talking...then dancing...then flirting. She was so fuckin' funny. I liked talking to her. We didn't exchange names...I called her Red and she called me Titan."

At that, Kathy barked out a laugh. "Sorry, but that name so fits you."

Pretending to scowl, he was unable to keep the grin from his face. "Anyway, we decided on one night. I took her to the downtown Hilton, and it was just supposed to be for a few hours." Chuckling, he said, "Damned if it didn't last all night. And then I wanted more. We agreed upon the weekend. Then, it was just too good. So, we gave ourselves a week. We'd meet in the evenings, after work and I'd been here. Still, no names and no regrets. That was our agreement."

"Oh, baby brother. That sounds like a recipe for disaster. A week of time together should involve names and can only end in regrets."

Blowing out a huge breath, he nodded. "I wanted her to come here last night. I...I needed her here, you know? I wanted more. But, then, when we got back and we were lying in bed, I began to think of all the reasons we wouldn't work."

Cocking her head to the side, she asked, "Like what?"

He spread his arms wide, "Like here. Like Cindy's needs. Like what family should be to each other... always available."

"Oh, my God, Cael. This...Cindy's illness and needs affects us all, but we don't stop living. I would never want that for you. Hell, if Cindy was older and understood more, she would never want that for you either."

"Well, it's too late now anyway. It was supposed to be our last night and she left early this morning, leaving a goodbye note on the table. Said it would be too hard to say goodbye in person."

"But..."

"Sis, I still don't know her name. Nothing about her life or where she works." Time crawled between them, each lost to their own thoughts, before he took the last sip of his coffee and said, "It's over. And you're right— the way it ended was a disaster, for me at least." Seeing the tears in her eyes, he stood and offered her hand to assist her up as well. Offering her a hug, he held her tight. "Come on. Let's go see if Cindy is awake."

Climbing down the ladder propped against the roof of Miss Ethel's house, Cael followed Zander and Jaxon to the ground. Asher and Jayden came down another ladder on the other side of the house. They had worked practically since dawn, spending Saturday morning re-roofing. Rosalie was at a teacher's conference that morning and Eleanor was spending the morning at the veteran's clinic she ran, so it was just the guys. Miss Ethel had called them to come down for lunch when a truck pulled into the driveway and Rafe and Zeke alighted.

"Got the rest of the roofing tiles," Rafe called out.

Cael nodded and motioned them inside, "Good timing. Food's ready." Entering the dining room, he rushed to take the tray of drinks from Miss Ethel's hands and set them on the table already laden with food —fried chicken, potato salad, green beans, homemade rolls, and peach cobbler. They all settled quickly, each filling their plates, making sure her plate was filled as well.

After a few minutes of the silence only being broken by the sighs of contentment, as they tasted the good food, Asher finally looked over and said, "So, you never finished your story."

When he realized Asher was talking to him, he looked up in surprise. Swallowing his bite of cobbler, he said, "Story? I told you all there was. I finally got my head outta my a...uh...outta the sand, and it was too late."

"So, you got nothin' to go on?" Zander asked.

Shaking his head, he replied, "Nothing. No name. No place of work. Not even what kind of work she does. I went by the bar where we met and the bartender remembered her...or rather her hair. Said he'd never seen her before that night or after."

"Can I ask why you thought you could not have a real relationship with her?" Miss Ethel asked, her warm, grey eyes on him.

Rubbing the back of his neck, he sighed heavily. "I don't know. Looking back, it seems stupid now. I'd been the one all week pushing for another night...another day. Then, I got that call from my sister and I actually wanted her to go to the hospital with me. But, as I spent time with Cindy, it just seemed so overwhelming. Cindy needs me. My sister and Tom need me. I just wasn't sure that there was room for another relationship. It didn't seem fair to her or to me, I guess."

"We have an endless amount of love to give," Miss Ethel said. They all turned their attention to her. "When George died, I assumed I'd be all alone. No children. No other family. I felt so empty inside. Looking back, I realize it wasn't from not having someone to love me. It was from me having so much love inside that I needed to give."

She smiled at each of them as they stared at her in unabashed admiration. "I loved each boy they brought to me, whether it was for a few nights, a few weeks or, like you, until you were grown." Settling her gaze back on him, she continued, "I know what your family is going through is heart wrenching and I'm not surprised that you sought someone to take your mind off your troubles." He blushed and she laughed softly. "Boys, I'm not a prude. I know you were looking for a physical... diversion. But, I'm also not surprised you found someone special. What I am so sorry about, is that you thought you didn't have room for all the people in your life, including someone new."

She stood from the table and every one of them stood quickly in respect, before sitting back down. She walked to his seat and placed her hand on his shoulder. As tall as he was, even sitting, she did not need to bend much to place a kiss on his cheek before adding, "I have no way of knowing what life holds for you, dear Cael. But, I'm sure that true love will find you. Perhaps, when you least expect it. Or, maybe…it already has."

11

"Regina! Oh, darling, it's so good to see you," Enrico called out as she walked through the large, glass doors into the beautifully decorated room. He was tall, with his hair trimmed at the sides with the longer hair on top swept up and back. Over the navy t-shirt and dark jeans he wore, his light blue silk shirt was open, the sides flapping out as he rushed to her. He air-kissed her cheeks with dramatic flair, before pulling her into a hug.

She laughed, hugging him in return, feeling the extra tightness of his arms around her. As she leaned back to peer at him, he blinked rapidly to quell the tears threatening to fall. "Now, now, none of that. Not today," she warned, shooting him a pretend glare. She knew this appointment was going to be hard enough as it was without his dramatics. Shaking her head, she chastised herself. *He's not being dramatic...as a friend, he feels this deeply too.*

She had glanced at her reflection in the storefront

windows as she walked along the downtown street, on her way to his establishment. Not a vain woman, she nonetheless noted her long hair swinging about her shoulders and down her back. As a child, she had kept her hair long as much as she could, her mother letting her keep it waist-length most of the time. In college, she did the same, often with the front pulled back with a clip, the thick waves falling down her back. Eventually, she had cut it a little shorter when she graduated, now keeping it where it hung at her bra strap, the color and fullness still eye catching. As she had peered at her reflection, she caught a few men walking by, turning to keep her in their vision, knowing it was her hair that usually caught their attention first.

Giving a mental shake to clear her mind, she settled in the salon chair, allowing Enrico to wrap the large, black cape around her body, fastening it at the neck.

"It's not too tight, is it?"

"Enrico, I'm not going to break. It's fine."

His eyes met hers in the mirror and she gave a firm nod. Answering with a nod of his own, he began to brush her clean, long, reddish-gold tresses into a thick pony-tail. Once it was fastened at the back of her head with a tight rubber band, he continued to wrap rubber bands along the length, every four inches, until a long, stiff ponytail hung in the back.

She noticed several patrons and stylists were eyeing the two of them, but she forced her gaze to the mirror in front. Licking her dry lips, she took a deep cleansing breath. He came around to the front of her and bent until his face was right in front of hers.

"I want you to be sure, Regina. It's not too late to back out."

"Enrico, nothing's changed. This has to happen. You know that. I know that. The only choice we need to make, is what to do with what we have."

He leaned further to kiss her cheek, this time his lips landing on the smooth surface, his voice shaky. "Okay, my dear, let's do this."

He moved behind her and, brandishing his scissors, held her ponytail in one hand while making quick work of cutting it off just above the top rubber band with his other. Within a few seconds, he held up almost twelve inches of silky hair. An assistant appeared from the side, taking the severed ponytail and placing it in a plastic bag and sealing it up.

She had assumed she would cry, but with the weight of her long hair gone, her head felt much lighter. Staring at her reflection, she recognized this moment represented so much more than her cut locks. It was a pivotal moment...a defining moment between her life before and what was to come. Lifting her gaze to his in the mirror, she gave a little smile.

He fluffed her remaining hair, curling in a bob above her shoulders. "You want me to shape this up and keep most of this length?"

His eyes held hope, but she shook her head. "You know the score, Enrico. You promised, when I called, to do what I asked. I'm sticking to the plan. It will make this easier. I need a new me."

He placed his hands on her shoulders and gave a

little squeeze. "All right, darling." With renewed vigor, his scissors began snipping at the locks once more.

When he finished cutting, highlighting, washing, and styling, he looked at her and smiled. "You are beautiful, Regina Nunzel, my dear. With your color, your bone structure...you can carry this off to perfection."

She stared at her reflection in the mirror with reverence. *The new me.* Her hair had been trimmed pixie-short all over, with a few more golden highlights in the natural red. Nodding, she smiled, both at herself and then at him.

With a flourish, he whipped the cape from her shoulders and she glanced down at the last of her old hair on the floor. An instant of sadness passed through her, but she pushed it away. Allowing him to pull her into a hug, she wrapped her arms around him tightly.

He whispered into her ear, "Thank you for allowing me to be the one to assist you with this journey."

"I couldn't have done this without you," she whispered back.

The assistant came back over, saying, "It looks beautiful, Ms. Nunzel." She held out the envelope with the bag of hair safely tucked inside. "I have the correct address on the envelope but wanted to make sure of the instructions that are to go with it."

"I have a change to make," she said, drawing a sharp look from Enrico.

"A change?" he asked, his brow lowered in concern.

"Change the delivery name and address. Use this one instead." She handed a piece of paper to the assistant.

"Cindy Clauson? Richmond's Children's Hospital?"

Smiling, she was proud that she remembered seeing Cindy's name on the white board in her hospital room. "Yes. This hair is for her. When you send it to the company, make sure to have that on the order form."

The assistant smiled and walked away to take care of the assignment, but Enrico whirled around. "What are you doing, Regina? What is this? I thought—"

Kissing his cheek, she said, "Sometimes, plans change. Sometimes, it's better to just love, even when there's no chance to have love in return."

Enrico stood, stunned, and watched Regina walk out of the salon, her head held high. His heart ached for the special client who had made more than one sacrifice that day.

Walking up to her townhouse, Regina was surprised to hear her name called. Turning around, she grinned as a handsome man jogged up the stairs behind her. Wearing a navy suit, with a crisp white shirt, he had loosened the tie at his neck. He was tall, but with lean muscles, not like—*nope, not going there.* His eyes crinkled at the corners when he smiled, but now, they were staring in wide-eyed shock.

"Hey, Robert. I didn't expect to see you this soon. You're off work early."

"I swear, I almost didn't recognize you," he said, his gaze fixated on the top of her head at her new hairstyle.

Giving her head a shake before realizing that the

short hair was not long enough to swing back and forth, she asked, "What do you think of it?"

He replied with a smile, "Honestly? It's different. Not at all you...yet, somehow, it is."

"I know what you mean. I felt the same when I saw my reflection also."

"And, while it'll take some getting used to, you're just as beautiful as always," he said, kissing the top of her head.

"Coming in?" she asked.

Nodding, he took the key from her and with his hand on her waist, led her into her home. Tossing her keys to the table by the door, he walked to the kitchen and, opening the cabinet, pulled down her teacups. Putting the kettle on, he turned and watched her settle onto one of the stools.

"I could have fixed my own tea, you know?" she said, a smile on her lips.

He winked before answering, "I know that, sweetie, but you look ready to drop. Tired?"

Nodding, she replied, "Yeah...what else is new?"

His gaze shifted to the top of her head, the super short hair standing on end. "You okay...about that?"

Chuckling, she said, "You can call it my hair...well, what's left of it."

"Why did you cut it now?"

She dropped her chin, staring at the tea cup he had set in front of her. "The timing seemed right. Less hassle—"

"Less hassle? You loved your long hair."

Lifting her shoulders in a slight shrug, she shook her

head. "I needed a change and the time seemed right." Taking a sip, she stared into his eyes, seeing concern in their depths. "It'll be fine, Robert."

He walked around the corner of the counter and, with his hand behind her neck, bent to kiss her forehead. "I hope so, sweetheart. I really hope so."

12

Cael stepped into Cindy's room, his heart sinking to see her thin body lying so still. Tom moved toward him, jerking his head, indicating they could talk in the hall.

His stomach knotted but, once outside, Tom immediately said, "The doctors are really happy with how she's doing."

Blinking in surprise, he cocked his head to the side, waiting to hear more.

"I know she doesn't look all that good, with the weight loss. That's actually their biggest concern right now...the weight as an indication of infection. They'd like to send her home soon, since she will have fewer chemo treatments over the next month, but want to make sure she can keep food down first."

"I thought she was on something for nausea," he said.

Nodding, Tom agreed. "They have her on anti-emetics intravenously, but want to try her on oral so that she can go home with them. If not, we can have a visiting nurse give them through her IV port." He hesitated for a second before adding, "Kathy is also learning how to handle her care once she gets home."

Scrubbing his hand over his face, he cursed, "Fuckin' hell." Looking at his brother-in-law's face, he said, "How are you doing? I mean, I ask Kathy all the time, but you're working full time and then spending every spare minute here."

Tom gave a rueful snort, "Like you're not doing the same. Working construction all day and then coming here in the evenings so Kathy and I can have a break." Jolting, he added, "Oh, I forgot to tell you that we'll get some help with that, thanks to you."

"Huh? Help?"

"Yeah. Kathy got a call today from Miss Ethel. She and some of your brothers and their women are going to help out."

Grinning, he was not surprised. "I'm glad, man. If anyone has the ability to make someone smile, it'll be Miss Ethel."

They sobered for a moment before Tom held his gaze and said, "You know, when I first met Kathy, I was surprised to learn that you'd been raised by someone else and she had stayed with your grandmother. Of course, she told me that Granny hadn't been able to take on both of you and Kathy was almost grown by then. But, still…it hurt my heart to think of you having to go into the system. She used to tell me of Miss Ethel, but I just didn't believe it. Now, after all these years of knowing you and her…I'm real glad you ended up with her."

"Hell, me too. God was looking out for me when I landed on her doorstep."

Tom swallowed hard, blinking several times before he added, "You're the best brother, brother-in-law, and uncle. We can't thank you—"

"There's no thanks needed among family," he said, his large hand resting on Tom's shoulder. "Miss Ethel taught me that."

Just then Kathy appeared at the door. "Everything alright?"

"No worries, sis. Now, you and Tom go have a nice dinner. I've got some stories to read."

"Mirror, mirror on the wall,
   who is the fairest of them all?"

Cael was reading Snow White, a children's version of the classic fairy tale, his voice dramatic as he got into the storytelling.

Cindy looked at the pictures and her face scrunched. "The queen had her head covered as well."

He looked down, having never noticed that the artist's renderings had the queen in a full headdress that covered all of her hair. He looked at her, wondering what was going through her mind.

Peering up at him, she said, "Do you think her hair fell out too?"

"Maybe it did," he said, carefully, not wanting to upset her. "I do know that if you had been asking the magic mirror who was the fairest, it would have had to say you are."

She grinned widely, her smile touching his heart as it always did. He continued to read.

"Snow White ate from each little plate and drank from each little mug. Afterward, because she was so tired, she lay down on a bed and fell asleep."

"I don't think she should have gotten into a strange man's bed," Cindy interrupted. "Do you?"

Instantly, he answered, "Certainly not." His mind wandered to Red and he felt the heat of blush rise over his face. *She really took a chance going with me.* His heart ached at the thought that she was no longer his to watch over.

Cindy saved him from his thoughts when she begged him to keep reading.

"I'll give you one of my apples, the old woman said to Snow White."

"Why did Snow White eat the apple given to her by the old woman?"

"Uh…I guess she was hungry. What do you think?"

"But, Mama always says that I shouldn't take something from strangers and since Snow White had never met the old woman before, that makes her a stranger." She peered up at him, her eyes large in her face. Grinning, she called out, "Stranger-danger!"

He jolted at the reminder of Red using those same words, then sighed. Rubbing his chin, he said, "Well, I guess no one ever told her about that. Or maybe the author of the fairy tale didn't know about it either."

Cindy pondered for a moment before adding, "Of

course, if she had turned down the poisoned apple then the story would have a completely different ending. She wouldn't have fallen into a deep sleep and there would be no reason for the prince to come kiss her."

Always surprised by what came out of her mouth, he nodded in agreement. "I never thought of it that way. I guess, sometimes authors have to put things in stories, just to make them turn out a certain way."

"After a short period, a prince traveling through the land sees Snow White. Enchanted by her beauty, he instantly falls in love with her."

"Is that how you felt about the lady with the pretty hair that visited with you? The one you called Red."

Taken aback, he opened his mouth several times, but no words came out.

"I could tell she was in love with you."

"What? She was in love with me? I don't think…how did you…"

Giggling, she made a kissy sound and then laughed again. "It was in her eyes, silly. I saw the way she was looking at you when you read to me."

Kathy and Tom walked back into the room, their faces relaxed and their eyes warm on the scene in front of them.

"What's got you giggling, sweetheart?" Tom asked, walking over to kiss the top of Cindy's little, turban-covered head.

"Uncle Cael is like the prince in Snow White. He fell instantly in love, enchanted by her beauty."

"What's this?" Kathy asked, her eyes darting between Cindy and him.

Cindy clapped her hands again, laughing. "With the pretty lady he brought to see me. The one with the pretty hair. And she was in love with him."

Standing, he shook his head, "You're a little goof."

She turned her gaze up to him, saying, "She promised she'd be with me. Why hasn't she come back?"

Hiding his grimace behind a tight smile, he responded, "Not sure, Cindy-loo. But, I'm sure she's thinking about you."

Giving hugs all around, he walked out, his mind whirling. Like they often did, Miss Ethel's came back to him. *"I'm sure that true love will find you. Perhaps, when you least expect it. Or, maybe...it already has."*

Climbing into his truck, he tried to push back the anger of Red breaking a promise to Cindy.

Regina was exhausted. She dragged herself home from work and walked into her townhouse, barely able to keep going. Tossing her keys to the kitchen table, she threw the mail next to them before dropping her purse onto the floor. Moving to the kitchen, she opened the refrigerator and took out the orange juice. After pouring a large glass, she drank it while leaning against the counter.

Looking down at the mail, she plopped into a chair and sorted through the envelopes. One caught her attention and she ripped it open eagerly. Reading the thank-you letter from Compassionate Creations, she smiled, feeling lighter than she had in days. She leaned back in her chair, her hand automatically rubbing over her head, her fingers sliding through the super short hair. Her gaze drifted out the window as the sunshine broke through the clouds. Closing her eyes, she tried to imagine what life could have been like if only things had been different.

The nights with him. His body over hers as his hips pumped into her. The way his eyes lit when she came. The way he linked his fingers with hers as they walked along. Movies and popcorn. The lake. His body curved around hers, spooning as they slept. The feeling of safety when he was near. His smile as his eyes roamed over her face.

Sucking in a long breath, she let it out slowly as the words he spoke out loud their last night together, and the reason she left, came back to her.

Some happily ever afters don't come true after all.

13

"Why didn't you want to keep seeing her? That's the part I don't get," Jayden said, pinning Cael with a sharp look.

The men were over at Cael's house, working on the new addition. He stepped over the stack of drywall and stood with his hands on his hips, huffing out a breath. On weekends, he worked to improve his house, still undecided whether to re-sell it for a profit or to keep it for himself. His friends would help when they could and today, they were all over to get the drywall up in the addition built onto the back.

The two-story addition included a master bedroom and bath on the second floor and a large family room on the first. They were almost finished with the drywall and then he would be able to do most of the work himself.

"At first, it was just fun. I needed a night to blow off steam." Shrugging his massive shoulders, he said, "Then, it was…okay, I know you assholes will laugh, but it was pretty amazing. Not just sex, but more." He glanced up, expecting to see smirks on their faces, but instead, saw understanding.

Rosalie walked into the house, bringing lunch from Grimm's Pub, and quietly handed it out to the guys while they talked.

"I began to think in terms of longer, but then we visited Cindy that night and the weight of everything came crashing down. Cindy's diagnosis...treatment... my sister and her husband's needs." Shaking his head, "I held her that last night and all I could think about was there was no more room for someone else. Then the next morning, when I woke up, all I wanted to do was tell her that I wanted her in my life."

"And she never gave you any indication where she worked or what she did?" Zander asked, wrapping his arm around Rosalie, giving her a quick kiss.

"No, I mean yeah. Sort of. We never talked about specifics, but..." His head jerked up, his eyes working as a sliver of a memory came back. "Wait. We were watching old movies, she's a Hitchcock fan too, and she made a comment about how it was sad that old films were disintegrating and how fascinating it was to restore them." Stalking around the room, energy pouring off him, he said, "I can't believe I never thought about that."

Rosalie jumped into the conversation, excited, "I had my AP English class do a paper on comparisons of novels to movies, particularly the older movie versions. One student included in his research some of the work that is being done at VCU with the digitalization of old movies from film. Something about it being part of the Library of Congress, and they have grants for some universities to do the work on their campuses."

Lifting his eyebrows as he picked up a large sandwich, Jaxon said, "Looks like you got a starting place."

"But, I've got no name."

"So, do a little stalking."

"Fuck, you know how huge the university is…spread out all over the place."

"She wouldn't be in that many places. If she works for the University, you can find out where the film studies department is," Rosalie said. Shrugging, she added, "It's a good starting place and I certainly don't mind helping you."

Nodding, the squeeze around his heart loosened for the first time in weeks. He had a plan. Walking over, he kissed the top of Rosalie's head before grabbing another sandwich.

Frustrated, Cael sat in his truck, for the fourth afternoon in a row, outside the Dramatic Arts building on the VCU campus. On the first day, he had wandered halls, finally finding an office with the door plaque stating it was Film Studies. Entering, he talked to the Dean's receptionist, who had not been forthcoming with any information about a possible employee resembling Red, who might work in their department. He respected the woman's dedication to employee privacy, but had no idea what to do next. *Sit here every day and see who comes in and out?* So far, that had been his plan. For an hour after work, but before he went to the hospital, he sat so that he could watch the street. Today, Miss Ethel was going to go read to Cindy, so he had extra time to sit and stare at the people coming and going from the building.

A coffee shop was across the street and he pondered going in and getting a cup. A late fall cold spell had hit and the idea of hot coffee sounded good.

Throwing his head back against the headrest, he wondered what he was doing when the memory of her blue eyes gazing into his hit him. Whether they had just made love, were walking down the street, were sitting in a booth eating, or laughing at a movie, her smile lit her eyes.

Just then, a woman walked out of the coffee shop, her tall, athletic build catching his attention. He narrowed his eyes as he studied her from the distance. With a long, confident stride, she was a little thinner than Red. She wore a knit cap pulled down low on her head with a bright red scarf wrapped around her neck. Her face was turned away as she checked the traffic before crossing the road so he could not see it. Even so, something snagged his attention…the familiarity of her walk maybe.

She came closer. Closer. Holding his breath, as though afraid the act of breathing would make her disappear, he waited until she was almost to the door of the building. His heart leaped—it was her!

Her hand reached for the handle, when someone from down the street called out, "Hey, Regina!" She turned toward the voice, a smile lighting her face. *Regina. Her name is Regina. My Red.* His hand hit the door handle, his body preparing to jump from the truck, when a man's figure came from the left, hurrying toward her.

From his vantage point, he watched as she leaned in, her arms around the man, and he bent toward her. With their heads still together, they talked softly as they smiled at each other.

Removing his hand he sat back, his heart pounding as a sinking feeling hit his chest. *She's with someone.*

"Hey, sweetheart," Robert said, his arms wrapping around her. "How are you?"

Smiling up at him, her hands resting on his shoulders, Regina said, "I'm fine. I just came from the coffee shop, but my break can last a little longer. Do you have time for some?"

"I'm sorry, no, but I'm glad I got to see you."

Nodding, she smiled, but her eyes were wary. "You look pre-occupied. How you are doing?"

Chuckling, he said, "I'm good…everything's good. Work is a little crazy right now." His eyes jumped to the building beside them. "Are you still on schedule to finish up here?"

"Yeah, this is my last week. Then, I officially get to work from home full time. Well, at least until I decide to come back. Who knows, I might like working from home."

He lifted his hand and touched her cheek before pulling her in for another hug. She rested her head on his shoulder, closing her eyes tightly as their arms circled one another. Time stood still for several minutes as they held each other. Finally, bending to her cheek, he kissed and let her go. "See you soon."

She nodded, blinking as the stinging behind her eyes hit. She cupped his jaw before waving goodbye and calling out, "See you later." A little stronger and a little weaker at the same time, she stood for a moment, watching him walk down the street.

Cael watched, his mind in turmoil, as Red turned to go inside the building, hesitating before opening the door. Her shoulders slumped and she swiped at her eyes before taking a huge breath. Standing straighter, she threw open the door and went inside.

He sat for a moment, concerned, wondering why she looked so defeated all of a sudden, when the realization that she was with someone reverberated through him again, blocking all emotions save one. Betrayal snaked through him before settling, coiled in his gut. *How the fuck could I have been so wrong about her?* Scrubbing his hand over his face, he tried to reason through his emotion.

Could she have hooked up with someone new since I saw her? They looked too intimate...too familiar with each other. Nah...she knew this guy. Angry, he reminded himself it had been just sex...*who gives a fuck if she was stepping out on her boyfriend.* Slamming his hand on the steering wheel, he knew what made the difference. She was no mere fuck to him. She was someone he had feelings for. Shit...*I took her to the hospital to meet my family.*

Irrational anger pored through him and he started his truck, pulling out into traffic. At the next intersection, he sat at the red light trying to calm down, when his attention was snagged. The man Red had been with was waving toward another car.

The car slowed and he jumped into the passenger side, then leaned over, kissing the woman behind the wheel. Confusion and renewed anger hit him and with no real idea what the hell he was doing, he changed lanes and followed the car.

Staying a few cars behind, he followed them to a quaint neighborhood, just on the outskirts of the city. He parked several houses down, keeping his eyes trained on the car. The man alighted first, and to Cael's great surprise, bent to the back seat, unbuckling a little boy. Gasping, he realized the man was a father. Staring, as his heart beat harder, he watched the woman step from the driver's seat, and he was able to see her pregnant belly. As the man reached his hand down to hold the little boy's, he saw the wedding ring on his hand.

Leaning his forehead on the steering wheel, he groaned. Red was seeing someone and that someone was married. The reality hit him...she not only cheated on her boyfriend with him, she was cheating on a cheater.

Cold filled the places in his heart that had burned warm for her.

14

Cael slumped on his sofa, comfortable in his sweat pants and old t-shirt, his boots kicked off at the door. Crushed, empty beer cans laid haphazardly on his coffee table. Not long ago, he had switched to whiskey, straight from the bottle. It took a lot of alcohol to get him drunk, but he was well on his way.

His alcohol soaked mind ignored the movie on the TV, instead sliding dangerously to his past. His thoughts wandered not to the good memories, and there had been plenty, but to the memories that threatened to choke him if he gave them too much room.

He had been five years old when three men, dressed in fancy military uniforms, had knocked on the door. His mother had begun crying as soon as she saw them, while he had clung to Kathy's hand, not understanding what was happening. He remembered looking up at her, seeing confusion on her face as well. The men had barely begun to talk when their mother wailed, dropping to the floor in a ball.

One of the men asked Kathy if there was someone who could come and she had mentioned one of their mother's friends. Soon, the house had been filled with friends and neighbors, all who clucked over their mom, shooing he and Kathy out of the room.

Kathy and he had hid in his room upstairs, the sound of their mother's cries ringing through the house. After a while, one of the neighbors came to get Kathy, talking to her in a soft voice outside the room. He had been curious, but fear kept him stuck on the bed. Afraid that Kathy might fall to the floor like their mother, he grabbed his bear and held tight.

Days later, he stood with his mom and sister, looking at the flag draped casket. They told him that his daddy had been killed. Looking at the framed picture sitting next to the casket, his father dressed in his military uniform, he had tried to remember everything he could about him. But, the memories, while good, were few. His dad had been overseas from the time he began kindergarten. Mom had told him stories of how brave his father was and how she fell in love with the handsome soldier, but they did little to help him remember.

Though it made him nervous to see her so distraught, he had snuck a glance at her that day, her face white and pinched, her eyes swollen and red. Unsure what he should do, he had looked to Kathy, who held his hand, and her face looked a lot like their mom's. He had wanted to cry, to be just like them, but it just seemed that his dad would be coming home soon, like he promised. He could not understand the finality of what had happened.

After the service, some men folded the flag and handed it to his mom. He had thought that was cool, the way they worked together to get the flag folded in a perfect triangle, but his mom must not have. She took the flag and then fell out of her chair, wailing again. People rushed around her, pushing he and Kathy to the side.

He took another long swig of whiskey, his memories from that moment, and from the next year, were the same. His mom on the sofa or in bed, either crying or sleeping. Kathy got him up in the mornings and ready for school. She made sure he took a bath at night and had food to eat. Barely a teenager herself, she managed to handle everything.

He kicked his sock-covered feet up on the coffee table, empty beer cans scattering in all directions, many dropping to the floor.

He remembered walking home from school one day, Kathy by his side, and turning on their street only to see flashing lights in their driveway. People coming in and out of their house. A neighbor running to intercept them. Kathy dropping his hand as she tried to run forward. A man holding her back.

He tilted the bottle up, draining the last dregs, as the visions continued passing through his mind. Another funeral. Whispers from those all around.

Years later, Kathy showed him their mother's death certificate. Accidental overdose. She had explained that because their mother had not left a suicide note, it was declared accidental. Alcohol and prescription sleeping pills.

He and Kathy never talked about it again, but in his eyes, their mother had abandoned them from the moment she learned their father had died, even though she lived in the same house. He had never been able to understand why she could so easily forget she had two children to care for and love. The idea that they had not been enough ate at him.

Standing, he staggered into the kitchen, looking for another bottle, only finding a forgotten, half empty bottle of whiskey in the back of a cabinet. Weaving back to the sofa, he fell onto the cushions, his head muddled from alcohol and memories.

Granny...old and tired. Saying she could take an almost grown granddaughter who could get a job and help out, but had no room for a little boy. Too much work raising a boy at her age. Once more, he felt the sting of not being enough for someone to care for.

His eyes lifted to the TV as a new, late-night movie began. Hitchcock's The Birds. *Fucking hell.* The reminder of his time with Red...*Regina*...hit him. Snorting, he grimaced. He no longer had to think about why she left that morning...*this time, not because I wasn't enough, but because she already had someone.*

As the opening credits rolled on the movie, he leaned forward and threw the bottle in his hand toward the screen. With his powerful arm, he heard the bottle and the TV shatter just before he slumped over, passing out on the floor.

"Jesus, it stinks in here."

Zander moved into the room, Jayden and Jaxon right behind him. They looked down at Cael, lying on the floor, beer cans surrounding him. A quick scan of the room also exposed the busted TV, while the smell of whiskey filled the air.

"Fuckin' hell," Jaxon cursed. "I like to tie one on, but never like this. And Cael, especially, never gets stinkin' drunk." He moved to open the windows in the living room and then in the kitchen to get a cross breeze. Jayden turned back to the front door, propping it open as well.

Zander squatted next to Cael's snoring body and rolled him over. "Let's get him in the shower and then get some coffee in him."

Considering his size, it took all three to get him up. Waking, he grumbled as they maneuvered him down the hall and into the bathroom. Leaving his clothes on, Zander held him in place with his hand pressed on his chest, forcing his back against the tile, and turned on the water.

As cold water sprayed from the showerhead, hitting Cael's face, he jumped, cursing as he sputtered. His hands came up, but Zander slapped them back down.

"Quit your bitchin' and stay there until you don't stink anymore. When you can see clearly enough to walk, get dressed and get some coffee in you." With that, Zander walked out and headed back to the kitchen.

Looking at the mess, he shook his head. "Jesus, what the fuck was he doing?"

"Could be Cindy or…you think it's that woman?" Jayden asked.

"Fuck this," Jaxon said. "All for some woman?"

Zander stood with his hands on his hips and sucked in a deep breath. "Got no idea. But something's happened. He never gets outta control. Never." Looking at the twins, he said, "Find some coffee and get it going. I'm calling everyone."

Thirty minutes later, Cael walked into the living room, now wearing a clean t-shirt, with his bare toes sticking out from underneath clean jeans. His hair stood on end where he had run his hands through the wet strands. He had not shaved, but his weekend stubble was a normal look for him. He scanned the room through bloodshot eyes and moved straight to the coffee mug, being handed to him by Asher. A bottle of aspirin sat on the counter as well. Popping the top, he shook out two and swallowed them.

Leaning his hip against the counter, he took a long sip from the black coffee, the bitter taste hitting him instantly. He hoped the caffeine would soon kick in as well. Peering out into his living room, the mess was still evident. He knew his friends cared but one of Miss Ethel's lessons was that if you made a mess, you cleaned it up. The idea was that you would be less likely to make the same mess again. Looking at the scattering of empty, crushed beer cans lying about the room, the broken whiskey bottle and the smashed TV, he sighed heavily.

Jayden and Jaxon were sitting on the sofa while Asher, still in the kitchen, leaned forward on his forearms on the counter. Rafe rested his back against the door and Zander sat in the other chair, one ankle resting on the opposite knee, looking casual, but he knew him well enough to know he was feeling anything but that. Zander's t-shirt still had wet spots from the shower spray.

Nodding toward the busted TV, Zander quipped, "Didn't like what was on? You can always just change the channel, you know?"

Slumping down on a kitchen stool as the others chuckled, he said, "Okay, let me get this out of the way first. I'm sorry as shit you all had to come over and see me like this. I know we were supposed to work on my house today and having to sober me up was not in the plans."

Zander shook his head and said, "Man, you don't gotta apologize to us. Hell, you don't even gotta tell us what the fuck is going on. We're here. We're gonna work on your house and you can clean up this mess."

Jaxon grinned, "We just don't want you around any power tools today. You got a hangover, you're liable to shoot one of us in the ass with your nail gun."

Everyone laughed and even he had to join in. Holding his aching head, he said, "Fuck, that hurts." Too tired to talk at length about his situation, he just nodded and said, "I'll get going in here and let you all start in the back."

The guys filed out of the room and he finished gulping the coffee before pouring another one. He rounded the counter and opened the cabinet with cleaning supplies. First grabbing a large garbage bag, he shook it open as he walked into the living room. Bending he gathered up the multitude of beer cans, not bothering, nor wanting, to count them. Next, he gathered up the large pieces of broken whiskey bottle, glad it had not shattered. Staring at the TV, he grew disgusted with himself. *Fuck, that was a good TV.*

Getting the vacuum, he sucked up the shards of glass and then continued to run it over the entire floor. Unplugging the TV, he hauled it to the street, placing it next to his trash can. Seeing one of his neighbors in their yard staring at him, he waved. "They don't make 'em like they used to." The neighbor's wide eyes stayed on the shattered TV as they nodded before hurrying back into their house.

Returning to his own house, he grabbed the cleanser and sprayed his coffee table, sticky with spilled beer. After scrubbing he stood back and surveyed his progress. Satisfied that he had returned his living room to its former appearance, sans the TV, he moved back into the kitchen. Opening the refrigerator he scanned the contents , but had no desire to make a bunch of sandwiches. Pulling out his phone, he called for pizza instead.

Ready to face everyone again, he headed to the back of his house, where he found them hard at work. The two-story addition now had the drywall finished and the men were working on installing the windows today.

"Thanks guys," he said, looking at what they had accomplished in the last hour. The master bedroom's large windows were in place, as was the smaller one in the master bathroom. "Pizza will be here in a few minutes. I want you all to eat before you leave."

By the time they finished putting away their tools, the pizza had arrived and they headed downstairs, finding the living room no longer resembling a trash heap.

Asher took a bite of pizza and then said, "Okay, no one else will ask, but I'm just gonna put myself out there. What the fuck happened to you last night?"

Leaning back in the deep cushions of his sofa he heaved a great sigh. "I found her."

"The woman?"

Nodding, he said, "Yep."

"Okay," Asher continued. "So, what happened that had you pickling your liver last night?"

"She's seeing someone else." He observed their wide eyes and added, "And the guy is married."

"What the fuck?" they all expressed in one way or another, their attention riveted on him.

Explaining what he saw and how it all went down, he finished with, "Basically, she was cheating on this guy with me. She probably figures cheating on a cheater doesn't matter."

Jayden chewed thoughtfully for a moment, then asked, "But you don't know for sure?"

"Huh?" Halting mid-chew, he stared at his friend, rearing back.

Shrugging, Jayden said, "So, he kissed her. Maybe he just works with her."

"You kiss the people you work with?" he shot back.

"I got all men in my garage...think if I tried to kiss them, I'd get punched," Jayden laughed.

Asher shook his head, adding, "Look, I think what Jayden's saying is that you don't know for sure." Throwing his hands up in defense, he continued, "You know what you saw, but maybe it's not what you interpreted. Maybe it is...but don't you at least owe her the chance to explain?"

Jaxon lowered his brows, saying, "He doesn't owe her shit, guys."

"Okay, then he owes himself the truth. At least, he'd know for sure."

Looking over at Zander, he cocked his head to the side. If anyone would give him the best advice, it would be him.

Zander's eyes held both intensity and fondness as he leaned forward in his chair. "Everyone deserves a chance. Assumptions are never good, especially when they concern something as important as the person out there that might be your other half. You admitted you felt something deep for her. Go back, Cael. At least give her a chance to let you know if she's what you hoped she'd be or not."

Sucking in a deep breath, he nodded slowly, both hope and fear warring inside.

15

Cael walked into Cindy's room, pleased to see her sitting up in bed, her color better than the previous days. "Hey gorgeous," he called out, smiling at her. Holding out both hands in fists, he directed, "Pick one."

Eyes wide, she giggled as she leaned forward, considering each of his large fists carefully. Tapping his right hand, he flipped it over, opening it, exposing another stretchy cap, this time covered in Tinkerbells.

"Oh, I love it," she squealed and his heart pinged at the excitement from this little girl over a cap that would keep her bald-head warm.

The unfairness of life hit him in the gut, but before he could reel from that, Kathy smiled and said, "Hmm, I wonder what would have happened if you picked the other hand?"

Cindy's attention turned back to him, now her wide eyes on his still closed left hand. Grinning, he flipped it open as well, offering another cap to her. This one had the princess from Tangled, the images of her with her shorter hair.

She threw her arms out wide and he stepped forward, encircling her frail body in his massive embrace. "Love you, sweetheart," he said, his voice gruff with emotion.

He looked at Kathy over the top of Cindy's head, seeing her mouth *Thank you*. Later, after hearing about Miss Ethel's visit and story time, he stood at the door with his sister.

"She looks good tonight."

"Yeah, she's had a good day. But, then, tomorrow is chemo day again so we start the cycle all over."

"Oh, fu—" He shook his head, correcting quickly, "I'm so sorry."

"We'll see how she does. They now have a better handle on her nausea, so my prayer is that it'll be easier than last time."

"Me too, sis."

She held his gaze and said, "I suppose you haven't heard from the woman who came here with you? The one you were falling for?"

Shaking his head, he decided to not let her know that he had found her, simply saying, "No. Why?"

"It's silly, but Cindy keeps asking for the lady with the princess hair. I've told her that she was a friend of yours but not a close, best friend you see all the time, but she insists that the two of you are in love." Shaking her head, she sighed. "Anyway, just ignore me. I know you two aren't seeing each other anymore. I swear, sometimes I feel like I'm losing my mind. Maybe I just wanted to hear something sweet happening with my baby brother in the midst of all this with Cindy."

He pulled his sister in for a hug, his gaze landing on the small girl in the big bed, machines connected to her humming away, as she played with her new caps. Irritation that Red had just walked out of Cindy's life after saying she would be back rolled through him.

Once more, Cael found himself sitting outside of the Dramatic Arts building. His stomach churned as he wondered what he would say. He did not have to wait long before seeing Red exit the building.

She walked a few feet before stopping to adjust the knit cap on her head and secure the scarf around her neck. Climbing from the truck he hesitated for a second, then jogged toward her.

"Regina," he called out, using the name the other man used.

Regina turned around, her eyes searching for a second for who had called her name before they landed on Titan. Stunned, she stared at the man she never thought she would see again. Her gaze devoured him as her heart pounded. Everything about him was familiar, from his strong jaw to his wide shoulders and chest, covered with a thick, denim jacket, all the way down to his worn jeans and booted feet.

Her mouth opened, but no words came out as her hand shot up, once more adjusting her cap. She had wondered what she would say if their paths ever crossed, but now, a strangled squeak was all that came out, afraid of him noticing the change in her appearance. Glancing back at the building, she never expected to see him standing in front of her workplace.

Cael walked the remaining few feet until he was standing close enough to see each freckle across Regina's nose. Her face, as familiar to him as his own reflection, appeared pale and her eyes larger than before.

Her lips curved into a slight smile as she peered up at him. "How...how do you know my name?" she asked, confusion in her eyes. Looking around for a few seconds, she added, "And, how did you know where to find me?"

"You said you worked with old movies. I did a little research. It seems there's not too many places that do that type of work."

Blinking, Regina glanced from him to the Dramatic Arts building, understanding dawning. "Oh..." She stepped forward, lifting her hand toward him, jerking in surprise when he backed away. Her smile dropped as she stared into his face, confusion still plaguing her.

"I need to ask you a question and I hope to God, you give me the truth. If not for me, then for Cindy."

"Cindy? Is she alright?"

"As well as can be expected. Of course, it's hard for a seven-year-old, dealing with cancer, to have to understand when someone makes a promise to visit and then they don't keep it."

"I...I'm sorry...but, we made no...promises...you and me...I..."

"No, you slipped out the next morning when I was still asleep. Fucking exhausted and you just left."

Biting her lip, knowing he did not realize she had heard his words whispered in the night, she said, "It seemed best. You had so much to deal with."

Nodding, he did not reply and the air between them turned colder. Unsure what to say, she waited.

"Tell me this...the man you were with the other day...the man you stood right here and hugged... kissed...did you know he was married? Married, with a kid, and a pregnant wife?"

She opened her mouth but a gasp was all that escaped. Eyes wide, she stared, stunned into silence, at his hard face. Her mind raced with the implication of what he was asking. *He was here...he spied on me...he knows my name...he thinks...oh, my God...he thinks that I was lying...* Pain slashed through her, and her hand shot to her stomach as she tried to quell the feeling of nausea hitting her. She sucked in another shuddering breath as her heart beat a staccato in her chest.

Cael's face was hard, as though carved in marble, as he stared back at Regina, his eyes glittering cold. He watched the play of emotions cross her face. Unable to identify them all, he focused on her wide-eyed, open mouth surprise. Nodding slowly, he stated, "So, you do know the man you are obviously so close with is married."

Regina's chest heaved as she swallowed audibly, his accusation filling her being in a terrible, aching way. Drawing herself up to her full height, she said, "Yes. I know all about him. I know he's married. I know he has a child. I even know his wife is pregnant."

He reared back, his cold eyes now glacial.

Taking in his expression she pleaded, "Don't you even want to know how I know all this?"

Shaking his head in disbelief, Cael stalked closer until he towered over Regina, noting she held her ground. He knew it was an asshole maneuver to use his considerable height to his advantage, but he was beyond caring. "No. I don't fuckin' care."

She gaped for a moment before clamping her mouth shut, confusion and softness replaced with determination and a spine of steel. Clenching her fists, she shook with anger.

"You won't even deny cheating on a cheater," he breathed out in disbelief.

"Why should I? You've already made up your mind." Shaking her head, she poked him in the chest, her finger right over his heart. "You know me. You might not have known my name when we were together, but you know *me*. And you think *this* of me? Judging me so quickly after all the time we spent together?"

He stared, her words catching him off guard. Giving her one last chance to explain herself he asked, "You got any other explanation for what I saw?"

A tear ran down her face and she swiped at it angrily. "I've got nothing to say to you. Nothing." Standing, pale and shocked, she blinked rapidly, refusing to speak.

Though she had her walls up, that tear struck a cord with him. *But I gave her the chance to deny what I saw. Two chances, in fact, and she didn't. She even confirmed she knew about that guy!* Firming his resolve, he said, "I was willing to ask for more, 'cause I thought what we had was real. My friends even convinced me that I needed to find you to see if there was more to us. God, I was a fool."

Done with everything, he turned and headed back down the street toward his truck, his mind in a whirl. Looking over his shoulder, he called out, "Honest to God, when I think of what that week meant to me... now, knowing I was a chump to think it meant something to you too? I guess for you, no regrets really meant no regrets."

With that, he threw open the door to his truck and climbed into the cab before gunning it down the road, leaving her standing on the sidewalk, unable to move. Regina slumped against the brick wall for several minutes until a passerby looked at her in concern.

"Miss? Are you okay?"

Startling, she pushed away from the wall and nodded. "Yes...uh...yes." They continued to stare for a moment before moving on down the sidewalk.

Uncertain of her steps, she walked zombie-like to her car, climbing inside and sitting with her hands on the wheel for a while. Finally blinking back to reality, she started the car and pulled onto the road. The entire way home, she showed no emotion. It was not until she walked up the steps of her townhouse and unlocked the door that she allowed her heart to take over her mind.

Every move she made felt like it was in slow motion. Closing the door, she heard it click as it shut, her hand remaining flat against its surface. A lump was lodged in her throat making swallowing difficult, but it was the sharp pain in her chest that had her lifting her hand, gently rubbing over her heart.

Her chin quivered and she tightened her lips in an attempt to quell the movement. Try as she might to hold it back, with the sob already caught in her throat, a quick inhalation brought it forth. A lone tear slid down her cheeks, falling unheeded on her shirt. Leaning her back against the door, her chest heaved as another sob left her body followed by more tears.

She had no idea how long she remained in that position, flattened against the door while her tears flowed. Blinking, she suddenly looked around, finally noticing her position. She wiped her tears, the slow burn of anger beginning to replace the pain.

Becoming an expert at ignoring pain, she pushed against the door and walked silently into her kitchen before opening the refrigerator. Pulling out the juice, she drank greedily. Wishing it were alcohol, she slammed the glass onto the counter, surprised it did not break.

"Damnit!" she screamed, her anger now morphing into rage. She had never meant for him to know of her sacrifice in the first place, but to have him, the man she had fallen for even though she knew he was unattainable, to berate her with such viciousness...*Fuck him!* She almost wanted to tell him what she had done for his niece just to see the look on his face when he realized what a dick he'd been. But no, that gift was for the little girl going through something so scary. It wasn't about the man who took her heart and then shredded it. Stomping through the house, she realized he knew her name and she still had nothing. No names and no regrets? *Well, that certainly bit me in the ass!*

As her anger stewed, she began to feel a bone-wearing fatigue. Slumping onto her sofa, she pulled the quilt over her, curling up on her side. With a shuddering breath, she willed her mind to still, hoping more sleep would come.

16

Cael was at work, earlier than normal. Unable to sleep, he finally left his house about five a.m. and had been at the worksite before six. The windows were in the condo he was in charge of and he was ready to install the floors. The space was voluminous, the living room and dining room one long area, broken only by the kitchen counter.

Hardwood floors would cover the entire space, including the kitchen. This unit already had owners, so they had final say in all the details. Ripping open the packing on the wooden planks, he measured and began laying the pattern out.

He liked working in the early morning, before his team arrived. The only sounds were those coming from the street below. What he did not like was the time it gave him to think. Think about Cindy. And, now, think about his conversation with Regina. It was not lost on him that he now knew her name but he had not given his. *It's not hers to have,* he thought, slamming a board into place with more force than needed.

He replayed parts of their conversation over and over in his mind while he worked. How she looked at him with pleading in her eyes as she asked if he wanted to know how she knew about the man's family. *Was she trying to tell me something or just deflect her actions?* Slamming another board in place, he grimaced. *I shut her down so I never learned if there was a reason. But what can the reason for adultery be? Nothing more than an excuse.*

He stood and walked over to the pallet of flooring, grabbing another armful to take over to where he was working. By the time his team began showing up at eight, he had half of the living room floor in place. Terrance walked in, took one look around and shouted, "Holland! Take a break!"

Standing, he shot him a glare but walked to him as the other workmen filed into the room, getting ready to start their day. Together, they walked out the door, into the cool, late fall air. Terrance moved to his thermos and poured a Styrofoam cup of coffee. Handing it to Cael, he then poured one for himself.

"Look, Terrance, I know what you're gonna say—"

"I seriously doubt that, Cael, but go ahead and spit it out."

Glaring at his boss, he said, "You're gonna tell me that I'm working too much, not sharing the workload, and my head is all over the fuckin' place."

"Is it?"

Blowing out a deep breath, he took a sip of the still-hot coffee and said, "Probably." Looking at Terrance, he said, "More than probably. My head *is* all over the fuckin' place."

"Your niece?"

"Yeah. It's going well according to the doctors, but she's got to stay in the hospital for her entire chemo treatments. So, what's good to the doctors doesn't always translate as good days for her."

"I'm sorry as hell, Cael. Real sorry. My wife's brother had to go through chemo and I know what a bitch it is."

They stayed quiet as they sipped more of the coffee, before Terrance said, "Anything else going on?"

Giving a rueful snort, he added, "Some woman I was interested in turned out to not be what I thought she was."

Chuckling, Terrance just nodded and said, "Sounds like you got a long list of shit that drove you to get most of the floor done by yourself this morning."

"Yeah, well, I couldn't sleep last night, so I figured I might as well pound out my frustrations on the floors."

Finishing the coffee, Terrance said, "To be honest, Cael, what I really wanted to talk to you about is a business proposal. That's why I wanted to get away from the others."

Curiosity had him leaning against the truck, his attention riveted on his boss.

"My uncle has his own construction company. Not like this," he waved his hand toward the large warehouse behind them, "but he does house restorations. His specialty is on old homes, restoring them to their former glory. Anyway, he had a heart attack and his wife is after him to slow down. I've got the opportunity to take over his business and I'm looking for a partner." He held Cael's gaze and said, "You're the best worker I've ever worked with. I also know you like doing the detail work. You've got talent and the eye for restorations. You're wasted on these big jobs, where skill is needed, but not talent. So, what I'd like you to consider is going into partnership with me."

"Working for you?" he asked for clarification.

Shaking his head, Terrance smiled. "No, not working for me. Working *with* me. Partners. Fifty-fifty. I know we can talk about the money aspect with lawyers at a later date, but I wanted to approach you first to get your feedback. You don't gotta let me know—"

"I'm in," he declared.

Terrance laughed. "Glad to hear it, but don't you want to know more of the specifics?"

"Absolutely, but the bottom line is that what you've just proposed is exactly what I've been wanting to do. These big jobs are okay, but I'd much rather work on restoration than these condos. So, you work up a proposal and let me take a look at it."

Finishing their coffee, they shook hands before he walked back inside, ready to continue on the floors, but his mind was on Terrance's proposal. *The chance to do special projects. Return old homes back to their former glory.* For the first time in days, a slow smile curved his lips.

That night, at Grimm's, Cael gathered his friends

around to celebrate his news. "Joe, serve 'em up," he called to the bartender.

The drinks and congratulations flowed. Looking at Rafe, he said, "I now know how you felt when you discovered you wanted to own your own business." Twisting around, he added, "And you, Zander, and you, Jaxon."

"It has its headaches," Zander said, "but it's nice to be my own boss."

"What projects will you be takin' on?" Jayden asked.

"He said we'd work on doing restoration projects. So, many of the old houses that need work, as well as some of the historical projects. For me, it'll be more craftsman work instead of the huge condo building."

As the server placed more pitchers of beer in front of them, he asked for a glass of water as well. The others lifted their eyebrows and he chuckled ruefully. "I'll have one beer, but I still have the nasty taste in my mouth from the other night."

As the evening continued, Grimm's began to fill and the music in the back continued to play. A brunette walked by, smiling at him with a wink.

"Interested in a dance?" she asked.

Her smiled widened as he stood, deciding to take her up on her offer. The woman was pretty enough, but there was nothing special about her. She did not capture his attention but, that was fine with him. He held her hand as they made their way to the back of the bar near the juke box, and he gave her a whirl as they began to dance.

"He's hurting," Jaxon commented, watching as Cael smiled at the woman without it reaching his eyes.

"He's got to figure it out himself," Zander said, his eyes on their friend as well.

Asher turned to him, tilting his head to the side in silent question.

Zander continued, "There's no substitute for heartache. No one can fill that hole. He's got to figure it out himself and then he'll be ready to move on."

After a few more minutes, Jayden, with a twinkle in his eye, stood and moved toward the back. Tapping Cael on the shoulder, he nodded toward the woman and, with a chin lift from Cael, moved in and began dancing with her. She shot Cael a glare before settling her eyes and smile on Jaxon.

Cael walked back to the table and sat back down, taking a swig from his beer. Seeing the others watching him closely, he looked at them in surprise. "What?"

"You gonna let Jayden cut in on your action?" Rafe asked.

Shrugging, he said, "Wasn't any action to cut in on. Just felt like dancing a little, but it wasn't like I was gonna put a claim on her."

"Still hung up on the woman who walked out on you?"

A flash of heat flew through his eyes before a touch of sadness replaced it. "No...yes...fuck, maybe." Snorting, he said, "Maybe I'm just not trusting enough right now to put myself back out there. Not even for a night."

"That's all?" Jaxon pressed.

He picked up his beer and Zander warned, "Don't be throwing that in my place."

Laughing, he shook his head. "Nah, man, just taking another drink." After a long swig, his mirth died and he said, "We'd agreed, no regrets. But, fuck it all, I have a lot of them. If my heart got involved, then that's actually on me, not her. For all she knew, I could have been with someone or hell, married and out for fun. But, I did fall for her and then took it out on her when I found out that she didn't get attached like I did. Looking back, I feel badly about that now…it was a dick thing to do."

He cast his gaze around the table at his friends and offered a sad smile. "Thanks for sharing a drink about my job news, but I think I'll head home now." With goodbye back slaps, he walked out the door. He drove around for a little while, the window rolled down and the cool, night air clearing his mind. As he pulled into his driveway, he was surprised to see Jayden sitting on his front porch. Getting out, he ambled up the walk.

Opening the front door, he motioned for him to follow. Once inside, he grabbed two water bottles from the refrigerator and handed one to Jaxon. Moving to the living room, they settled in chairs facing each other before he spoke. "What's on your mind?"

Jaxon, the more serious of the twins, said, "You know our mom died when she gave birth to us."

Staying silent, he nodded, waiting for Jaxon to continue.

"What you might not know is that she was an addict. Jayden and I had no idea until years later when our aunt, who took us on for a while, was getting married and her fiancé didn't want to be saddled with raising two boys whose, and I quote the asshole, 'mother was a crack whore'." Giving a rueful snort, he shook his head. "Had no idea what a crack whore was at that age. We later asked our aunt who, at least having the decency to appear embarrassed about the comment, just told us that our mom used drugs and had told her she had no idea who the father was. She cared about us, but not as much as her fiancé I guess, and that's how we ended up in the system."

"Shit, man," he responded, grateful he at least had a family photo from when he was little and everyone was happy. "I didn't know about all that."

"Sometimes I think Jayden chases tail just because he's horrified at the idea of falling for someone and having them leave him. Me? I play it safe, hoping one day I'll find what Zander and Rafe have, but got no idea if that'll ever happen. Doesn't mean I'm not a flirt, I just don't want to get serious."

He didn't know why Jaxon was unburdening himself, but he respected his friend enough to let him talk.

Jaxon took a long swig of water before speaking again. "You had something with that woman. Don't know what and don't know why she was doing what she was doing, but don't doubt yourself. Don't kick yourself that you were giving your heart to her. Makes you human...makes you a man." Standing, he said, "Just wanted to say that."

Cael stood and gave him a hug, glad that Miss Ethel taught them that real men hugged and were not embarrassed about it. "Thanks for sharing that, man. I had no idea." Slapping him on the back, Jayden nodded and headed for the door. He walked him out and watched him drive away from the porch.

Closing and locking the door, he turned off the lights and went upstairs. The back wall was covered in plastic, dividing the older part of the house from the newer, unfinished addition. Moving to the bathroom, he climbed into the small shower and let the hot water pound his tired muscles. With a towel hanging low on his hips, he stood and stared at his reflection in the mirror.

Jaxon's words came back to him. *"Don't kick yourself that you were giving your heart to her. Makes you human... makes you a man."* He did not regret giving his heart to Regina. His only regret was not getting hers back in return.

17

"You want to tell me what's wrong?" Robert asked, his arm around Regina as they sat on the sofa in her living room. She twisted around, so that he could observe the grimace on her face.

"You mean besides the obvious?"

Nodding slowly, he gave her shoulder a squeeze. "I can tell when you've got something on your mind and you have for weeks. Something's off but I can't figure out what. I know what I think it might be, but I'd rather you tell me."

She sighed, knowing he was right. She should tell him...with everything on his mind he deserved honestly.

Shifting slightly, so that she faced him with her leg tucked up underneath her body, she began. "You remember when you were out of town with your family?" Not waiting for an answer, she continued, "I went out. I went to a bar, just to have some drinks and some fun. I just wanted to forget everything...all the pressures, all the worries." Closing her eyes tightly, she could still see the moment her eyes landed on him. *The giant. Her Titan.*

"And..." Robert prompted, his eyes pinned on her face.

"And, I met someone." She opened her eyes but his face was closed off. Clearing her throat, she said, "We agreed...one night...no names...no regrets."

He nodded his head in slow motion before saying, "The phone call, telling me where you were?" She nodded and he did the same, in understanding. "Right. Okay. That seems fair."

Lifting her shoulders in a shrug, she said, "But the next morning, he wanted more. I did too. So, we changed the agreement to the weekend. Same rules applied."

"The whole weekend? You spent the whole weekend with him?" he asked, his brows, as well as his voice, raised. "That's not like you."

"I know...but there was a pull. Something magnetic about him, that I responded to."

Robert sat quietly for a moment, his face still unreadable. Finally, breaking the silence, he asked, "So, what happened at the end of the weekend?"

Sucking in her lips, she said, "We agreed to keep seeing each other for the rest of the week, in the evenings after work."

Blowing out a breath, he said, "So, that's where you were."

"Robert," she pleaded for understanding, "you've got your family. You've got responsibilities. I wanted something just for me and for the first time in a long time, I had that."

"Are you still seeing him?"

Shaking her head, she replied, "No. We went our separate ways, but after I had already realized my heart was involved, so it hurt. And then, I ran into him the other day…he came by my workplace—"

"Are you kidding me? Do I need to—"

"No, no, Robert. It wasn't like that. Don't worry, he won't be by again. But, we did talk for a moment and he proved to not be the man I thought he was, so that hurt too."

He wrapped his arm around her shoulders, pulling her in tightly. "I'm sorry," he said, his voice sincere.

"Yeah, me too." Settling in his arms, she heard his phone vibrate.

After he checked his messages, he turned toward her, but she was already standing.

"I know," she admitted, a smile on her face that did not reach her eyes. "You've got to get home."

He kissed the top of her head, as he mumbled, "Love you," before walking out the door.

Sighing heavily, she watched him walk down the street to his car and drive away. She closed the door with a resounding click, her heart aching for a love that was never to be.

A week later, Cael stood with Terrance, signing off on the initial paperwork for them to take over his uncle's construction business. There would still need to be meetings with a lawyer and bankers, but he grinned as they shook hands, knowing his life was about to take a dramatic turn. *Part owner in my own business.*

"You good, man?" Terrance asked, his smile firmly in place.

He chuckled, "Oh, yeah. Ever since you first brought this to my attention, I've been ready. In fact, I hadn't realized how much I wanted to do this kind of work instead of the newer builds until you suggested it. Now, I drive down the road and see houses that could use our special kind of skills."

"I know what you mean. Same here." Terrance folded the papers and put them back in his clipboard. "I'll get these to the lawyer and then we can start the proceedings for the business. We should be ready soon."

With a nod, he was walking toward his truck when his phone vibrated a message from his sister.

Come to hospital as soon as you can.

His heart jolted and he stood still for a second, horrible images flashing through his mind. Shaking his head, he ran the few feet to his truck and jumped in. Backing out, his tires squealed as he pulled out of the site's lot.

Rushing into the hospital a few minutes later, he tried to still his racing heart, but his mind would not shut down the possibilities. Fearing the worst, he grabbed his ID badge and hurried down the hall. He donned his gown and scrubbed up, finally making it to her room. With his mask in place, he halted at the door with his hand flat against the metal. Closing his eyes for a moment, he prayed for Cindy and for his own strength.

With a gentle push, he entered the room, his eyes darting all around, taking in Tom before landing on the empty bed.

Skidding to a stop, he gasped, "Where…"

Tom's face broke into a wide smile as he nodded toward the bathroom door, just opening. Kathy walked out first, her smile just as large as her husbands. "Cael! You're here." Turning to look behind her, she said, "Cindy, come show Uncle Cael what you got today."

He watched, dumb-struck, as Cindy walked out from behind her mother, her eyes wide and a huge grin on her still-pale, thin face. Instead of the colorful scarf on her head, she sported thick, shoulder-length, reddish-blonde hair. Blinking several times, as though the vision would change, he stared incredulously.

"Surprise, Uncle Cael!" Cindy shouted, her smile wide and her eyes sparkling. "Look at me!" She climbed up onto her bed, tucking her sock-covered feet underneath the covers as Kathy pulled the blankets up around her waist.

Still unable to speak, his feet moved of their own accord, taking him closer to the bed. The wig was perfectly made, easily matching her normal hair in color, although thicker. Shaking his head, he turned toward Kathy, questions in his eyes.

Shrugging, she said, "We have no idea who sent it." She turned, bending to the chair behind her and lifted a large box, now containing an empty Styrofoam head. "This was delivered today, specifically to Cindy. It's from Compassionate Creations. Tom looked them up on the internet and they create wigs and will make them from your own hair or the hair from a loved one."

"But…how…who…"

Still smiling, she replied, "We don't know. Tom called the company, but they wouldn't tell us any specifics. They only said that an anonymous donor had the wig made and the directions were to send it to Cindy Clauson at this hospital's address."

His mind raced but the obvious solution to the mystery was impossible to discern. He looked at Kathy, who was staring down at her gleeful daughter. Glancing down at Cindy, she was now busy playing with a doll.

"Do you know who I think I look like now?" Cindy asked him, turning her attention from her doll up to his face.

"No, baby. Who?" He smiled, sure she was going to mention one of the Disney princesses.

"I look like the pretty lady who came to see me when she was with you. This looks like her hair."

Shaking his head, he said, "No. There's no way."

Tom stepped up, his arms around Kathy and said, "You brought her here. She must have found out."

"No," he continued, more softly. "We didn't do last names. She couldn't have known."

Tom pointed to the white board on the wall, Cindy Clauson clearly printed at the top next to Patient. "She could have seen that."

A vision of Regina standing on the sidewalk outside her work building, tugging a knit cap firmly down on her head, floated into his mind. It had not hit him at the time how it would have been impossible for her to get all her long hair up under such a tight cap. *She cut her hair...for Cindy?*

Still shaking his head in disbelief, he said, "But why? Why would she do this for her?"

"Cael, only you can answer that. You said she was special. We just didn't know how special."

He looked back down at Cindy as the sun streamed through the window, illuminating the reds and golds in her hair. The more he stared, the more he knew Regina had to have donated the hair for the wig. It was the same play of colors in the light that he had memorized during the week they had together. That glorious, memorable week.

Her words from that night here in the hospital, when Cindy asked if she would come back, slammed into him. *"Yeah, baby. I'll be with you."* His heart ached as he realized this was what she had meant.

He reached out, his hand shaking, and touched the silken strands. The very same strands he had run his hands through. The feel of the tresses sliding over his fingers was an exact memory. His breath caught in his throat as tears hit his eyes. *God, it's hers. Her hair.*

"Isn't it beautiful, Uncle Cael?" Cindy asked, tossing her head back and forth, the silky hair swinging around her shoulders, as her wide smile penetrated his thoughts. "I'm just like a princess again."

Swallowing, he lost the battle as a tear slid down his cheek. A tear for his beautiful niece, fighting a battle no child should have to fight. And, for the woman who touched them all, but he had pushed her away.

"Let me get this straight," Jayden said, his mouth, normally in a wide smile, hanging open in shock. "This woman, the one that you met, banged for a week—"

"Jesus, Jay," Jaxon barked, kicking his brother under the table as Cael growled and Miss Ethel lifted her brow.

"Sorry...that's not what I meant," Jaxon said, backtracking, shooting Miss Ethel an apologetic grimace. "I mean, this woman you met and spent time with for only a week, cut off her hair to have a wig made for Cindy?"

"That's the only thing that makes sense," he said.

He looked at the others as they sat around Miss Ethel's large table, gathering for their weekly shared meal, each staring at him in shock. "I know it sounds crazy, but the wig came specially for Cindy from a company that makes wigs. I looked them up. They'll make wigs from someone's own hair. Like, if someone had cancer, knew they were going to lose their hair, they could have it cut and this company would make the wig out of their own hair. Or, hair from a family member or friend. In other words, they'll make a wig for someone specific."

"I still don't get why she would do that," Jaxon said. "Most women are real vain about their hair. Cutting it's a big deal. Cutting it almost all off is a big fuc—uh...big deal."

"Hair grows back," Eleanor said, leaning against her chair, Rafe's arm protectively around her shoulders.

"She gave something of herself, something that she could give."

"And Cindy is special," Asher piped up, as he finished the piece of pie placed in front of him. "The woman visits with you, observes a child in need and, even though you and she aren't going to keep seeing each other, she decides to give in a really personal way. It's pretty amazing, if you ask me."

"I know it is," he admitted. "I just don't know what to do about it. When I saw her last, I was upset about her seeing me while she was with someone else. I made it very clear what I thought about her at the time," he finished quietly.

Wincing, Jayden said, "It's kind of hard to come back from that."

"Tell me something I don't know," he groused.

Zander, staring at him, his face unreadable, finally said, "So...what are you going to do?"

He rubbed the back of his neck, willing the tension to go away. "I don't know. I mean, I've got to find her again. She deserves to know that Cindy got the wig and loves it. And, of course, that the family is grateful."

"And..." Zander prodded.

Sighing, he said, "I was a royal prick." Looking at Miss Ethel, he said, "I'm sorry for my language, Miss Ethel, but I was. Who did I think I was, being so sanctimonious?"

Miss Ethel's lips curved in a gentle smile. "Don't worry about a few curse words thrown out here and there. My George was a wonderful man, but he could cuss like a sailor when the occasion called for it."

Shooting her an appreciative grin, he continued, "We went into our agreement with no preconceived ideas of who we thought the other person was. It was just supposed to be...physical. But, when my feelings got involved and I found out that hers weren't, I acted like an ass. She didn't break our agreement...I did. But, I turned it around, acted all holier-than-thou. Hell, if she lays eyes on me, she'd have every right to kick me to the curb and I couldn't blame her."

"So, tell her that," Miss Ethel said, her eyes pinned on him.

He looked at her with doubt, before sliding his gaze around the table again. He knew she was right.

"It sounds like both of you made some assumptions and probably both made some errors in judgment. But, you can't control someone else's behavior. All you have control over...is you. You boys know what I always said —the measure of a man is not in the mistakes he makes but in how he handles those mistakes." She held him with her soft grey eyes, peering at him over her glasses. "Seems like you need to talk to her. It might not lead to the outcome you hoped for, but you can give her your apology and your thanks. The gift to Cindy is, after all, priceless."

Nodding slowly, he said, "You're right. I need to find her again."

Cael sat outside the Dramatic Arts building for two mornings and two afternoons but did not see Regina. He waited in his truck for a while, then in the coffee shop. Finally, he just went inside, avoiding the receptionist he had talked to before, instead staring at the floor directory, seeing Restoration Studies was on the third floor. Climbing the stairs, he walked out into the hall, seeing various people standing around talking and others going in and out of doors.

He stopped, uncertain what to do next. A woman with short, dark hair and almond eyes walked up to him with a smile on her face. "You've got to be new around here. Hell, I would have noticed you before!"

Her smile was infectious and he grinned in return. "I'm actually looking for someone. Regina? She works in film restoration, I think."

"Um…" she scrunched her nose as she thought.

"She had really long, reddish-golden hair—"

Her eyes brightened and she gushed, "Yes, of course. But, you've missed her, I'm afraid."

"Oh, is she gone for the day?"

Shaking her head, she said, "No, she doesn't come here anymore. I think someone said she works somewhere else...or maybe at home. Anyway, you won't find her here." Grinning up at him, she said, "Are you sure I can't help?"

"Thanks, but she's the one I need."

"Darn, just my luck," she said, laughing. "Hope you find her."

Thanking her, he admitted, "Yeah, me too."

Walking back out of the building, he sighed, wondering what his next step should be. As he sat in his truck, he sighed again. There was one person who would know where she lived—the man she was involved with. Banging his head against the headrest, he grimaced. *Fine...I'll talk to him tomorrow.* Clearing his mind, he started the truck and headed to work.

Sitting in his truck the next day, just down the street from the house he followed the man to a few days ago, Cael was thankful that he and Terrance had finalized their legal paperwork and turned in their notice to the construction company they had been working for. They had another week before they began taking over for his uncle so he had free time.

His eyes caught movement and he watched as the man came out of his house and kissed his wife on the front stoop while patting her stomach. Grimacing, he pulled out onto the road, following him. For a second, he wondered what he was really doing. *Following some guy like I'm in a fuckin' movie.*

Then, he focused on Cindy and her excitement over her new hair every day when he saw her. She smiled more. Laughed more. She integrated with the other children on the unit more. It was like she gained part of herself back that the cancer had taken. With that thought in mind, he no longer cared that he was following the man Regina was involved with. *As long as he gives me what I need, I can make amends for being a jackass.*

He stayed behind him all the way into the city, managing to keep him in his sights in spite of the early morning traffic. The man parked on a side street and Cael slid into an open space nearby. Climbing out of his truck, he sucked in a deep breath as he watched the man walk into a storefront office. Stopping on the outside, Cael observed the sign on the door.

Robert Nunzel, CPA, Accounting Firm

Throwing open the door, he saw the man standing at the receptionist's desk, chatting with a silver haired woman sitting at the desk.

She turned to him, a smile on her face and asked, "May I help you?"

His gaze shot between the two of them before he replied, "I need to speak to Robert."

Robert turned toward him and cocked his head to the side. "I'm Robert. What can I do for you?"

"I'd like to talk to you about Regina." He watched as

Robert blinked slowly, his brow lowering in confusion. "Privately, if you don't mind."

"Okay," Robert agreed, glancing at his receptionist. "Ms. Jones, please hold my calls."

"Of course, sir," she responded, efficient but with her gaze pinned on Cael.

Robert turned and moved down a hall, stepping inside a large office and moving behind his desk. Sitting down in a leather chair, he motioned for Cael to sit as well. He opened his mouth, then closed it quickly, appearing to wait for him to speak first.

"I'll make this quick," Cael said. "I need to see her and need to know where she lives."

Jerking, Robert said, "What makes you think I would tell you where she lives? I don't know you at all."

"I'm...well, I was a friend of hers."

"Was?"

Inhaling sharply, he nodded. "We became friends, but I'm afraid I left things...not good. I'd like to apologize, but don't know how to reach her."

Robert sat quietly, staring for what seemed like forever. Neither of them spoke. Just as Cael thought he was not going to say anything, Robert narrowed his eyes, saying, "You. You're the one who broke her heart."

Eyes wide at his choice of words, he clamped his jaw tight.

Robert continued, his voice hard. "She told me. Told me she met someone special when I was out of town with my family."

At the word *family*, he jerked, surprised the man had

the audacity to speak of Regina and his family in the same breath.

Continuing, Robert said, "She said things ended badly." Leaning forward, his words clipped, he added, "She didn't need that…not on top of everything else."

He wanted to roar that he would not be lectured by a man cheating on his wife, but he held his tongue. Inhaling a deep breath through his nose, he let it out slowly, his lips pinched. *This is about me…my atonement, not this guy.* "I was wrong for reacting the way I did. I need to tell her that." Swallowing hard, he added, "Plus, she did something incredibly giving for my family and I need to thank her in person."

Robert stared at him, again, for a long time. Fighting the urge to growl rudely, Cael held his stare. Finally, Robert let out a sigh and said, "I can't give you her address…not without her permission. That wouldn't be smart. You gotta see that. But, I can tell her that you came by and want to apologize."

Unable to hold back a sigh of relief, he nodded. He would not have given out a woman's information either. As he stood, his eyes landed on a framed picture on Robert's desk. Robert, his wife, their son, and…Regina. Staring, struck dumb at the sight of the picture, his gaze shot back to Robert's face. Having noticed the direction of his eyes, he too had looked at the photo, and was now smiling proudly at the picture.

Taking him in more fully, Cael noticed that, though Robert's hair was light brown, he had a smattering of freckles across his nose just like Regina. In fact, they had the same nose, and their eyes were also similarly shaped. The familial resemblance hit him like a ton of bricks and his legs gave out, causing him to plop back into the chair.

"That's a good picture," Robert said, not noticing his bewilderment. "Regina insisted we have one taken each year and my sister's very convincing. Plus, she loves her nephew and can't wait until she gets a little niece in a few months."

"Your...your sister?" he gasped, his gut clenching.

Robert's smile left his face as he stared hard at him once again. "My sister's had a hard time lately, and the last thing she needs...or I'll allow, is for her to be upset."

Nodding, he stood and offered his hand. "I promise I'm not going to make your sister's life any harder. I just want to apologize...for so many things, it turns out, and give her my thanks."

"She'll have her phone off while she's working, so I won't be able to talk to her until tonight. Who should I tell her came by? I didn't get your name."

"Titan. Just tell her Titan came by."

Cael sat in his truck for a long time, not moving, just staring at nothing as his thoughts swirled. He lifted his hand and rubbed his chest, the pain so real as he tried to massage it away. *What the fuck did I do? How the hell do I make this better? How the hell do I atone for such a major fuckup?* Usually a man of decision, right now, he had no idea what to do. *Maybe I should leave her alone. Let her get on with her life.*

The more he thought of that, the more he knew it was not what he was going to do. It might be selfish, wanting to apologize, but he knew it needed to happen. *She may not want to have anything to do with me but, hopefully, she won't hate me.*

Starting his truck, he drove, with no particular destination, his mind on autopilot. Coming to an intersection, he looked over, realizing he was at the park where they had spent time. Jerking into a parking spot next to the curb, he climbed down and began to walk. Hands in his pockets, he was impervious to the chilly wind as he followed the sidewalk trail toward the lake. Sitting on a bench, he stared into the water, watching the ducks paddling along.

"Ducks look so calm on the top of the water, but underneath, their feet are paddling like crazy."

"You know me. You might not have known my name, but you know me. And you think this of me?"

"You. You're the one who broke her heart."

"She told me. Told me she met someone special."

The weight of the memories hitting him had him bending over, the heel of his palms digging into his eyes, pressing against the sting of tears. He sat for a while, even though he knew self-recrimination would get him nowhere.

Pulling out his phone, he started doing a search on Regina Nunzel. It did not take long to come up with an address. *Fuck.* He was both relieved and unhappy that it was so simple. *Most women have no idea how easy it is for them to be found.*

Standing, he walked briskly to his truck, a destination now in his sights.

Cael drove along the street, peering out the window at the rows of brick townhouses in an older, but revitalized, area of town. He recognized that the houses were over a hundred years old, but someone had done an excellent job of reconstruction. As he glanced up and down the street, he saw families pushing strollers, young couples walking by, several older people mingling with young professionals. Nodding in approval, he appreciated the renewal of the older buildings and neighborhood.

He slowed down, coming to her block. Passing one with a bright red door, he grinned as he saw her street number painted over the door. *So like her,* he thought, then, shoved that thought aside as he remembered why he was here. *Will she talk to me or slam the door in my face?* He parked and sat in his truck for almost half an hour, battling with himself. The desire to thank her for what she did for Cindy was still first and foremost in his mind, but his previous behavior sat heavily in his gut.

Finally, he jumped down from his vehicle, his steps sure. Approaching her door, he sucked in a deep breath before letting it out slowly. The name on the mailbox said R. Nunzel. *Regina. My Red.* Lifting his hand, he hesitated for a second, then knocked sharply on the painted wood.

After a few minutes, when he had not heard any noise from inside, he knocked harder. Finally, he heard a slight shuffling just before the door latch clicked. The door swung open and there she stood.

She was wearing yoga pants with a slouchy, long sleeved, light blue t-shirt. Her super-short hair was sticking up on the side like she'd just been sleeping on it. Her face was pale and her eyes appeared large as she stared up at him, her mouth slightly open.

Neither of them spoke for a second and, then, she visibly startled, as if just recognizing who he was. Her eyes jumped to his and, seeing him staring at the top of her head, she sucked in sharp breath, her hand instantly flying to her hair, fingertips rubbing through the shorn locks. "I...uh..."

"Hey," he said softly, his gaze dropping back to her face. Now that she was in front of him, his words became stuck in his throat. The sadness in her beautiful eyes gutted him.

Licking her dry lips, she held on to the door handle with her left hand while her right hand dropped from her hair to fiddle with the bottom of her t-shirt. "Uh... how did you find me?"

Noticing her white knuckles clinging to the door, he rocked back a step. He did not want to overwhelm her or make her feel intimidated. He had used that tactic once, to his great shame. He would not do it again. And as much as he wanted to swoop in and hold her tight, he knew he no longer had that right.

"It's kind of a long story," he said with a chuckle, but the glare she gave him caused the hopeful mirth to die in his throat. Shoulders slumping, he replied, "How I found you doesn't really matter right now, Red. It's what I need to say that is important."

She lifted her eyebrow, her face unsmiling. "I think that the last time we met, you said everything there was to say."

"No," he all but shouted, his hand thrown up to stop the door from slamming in his face. "I totally fucked up and need...I need to apologize." He saw the doubt in her eyes as they narrowed and pressed his case. "I was wrong...so fuckin' wrong, to say to you what I said." She bit her lip and he added, "Please, let me talk to you. Let me apologize."

She hesitated, her face full of indecision. Dropping her gaze to her bare toes, she heaved a sigh. "I have no idea why I would even consider listening to you. I don't even know—"

He climbed back to the top step and thrust his hand out toward her, saying, "I'm Cael. Cael Holland."

Regina stared down at Titan's—Cael's— extended hand for what felt like forever. Thinking over everything that had happened...*offering forgiveness doesn't mean I have to let him back in my life, and life is too short to carry anger around. But, putting my heart out there again? Not sure I want to do that.* Without looking up, she slowly raised her hand and placed it in his. As he closed his hand around hers, she felt that familiar tingle, but pushed the feeling down. Lifting her eyes, she said, fatigue lacing her voice, "I'm really tired, Cael."

Cael's eyes searched Regina's face, observing just how pale her complexion was, the deep, dark circles under her eyes and concern hit his gut. "Then let me in, Regina. Let's sit down. I'll fix you some tea. I just need to apologize. I'm not asking for anything. I just...I was an ass and I can't believe I...you didn't deserve what I said to you and I'd like to make it right."

The look in Cael's eyes was so sincere that Regina found herself nodding slowly, replying, "Then I suppose you'd better come in, Cael Holland." Stepping back, she watched as he moved through her door, his large body seeming to fill the space. Closing the door behind him, she skirted around him and walked into her living room.

Looking around, Cael smiled softly, seeing so much of Regina in how she adorned her home. She had decorated in soft grays and blues, giving the space a clean, open feel. An exposed brick wall surrounded a fireplace, with a flat screen TV mounted above. On the opposite wall, between the tall front windows, sat an overstuffed sofa, with an abundance of purple throw pillows and a few purple blankets draped over the chairs. One was wadded up on the sofa as though she had just crawled out from underneath it. Two chairs sat at either end of the room and a large, braided rug brought the colors of the room together, while at the same time warming the hardwood floor.

She moved to one of the chairs, curled her legs up and wrapped her arms around her knees.

He observed her position, recognizing it for what it was—her protective stance. Walking to the sofa, he sat, sinking into the comfortable cushions. He wiped his hand on his jeans, all his practiced words leaving his mind.

"You wanted to talk…" Regina prompted, adopting what she hoped was an impassive expression, even while her stomach quaked.

Nodding, he said, "I…I need to explain. About so many things." Looking down at his hands, he sighed, "Fuck. I don't know where to start."

She watched his bowed head and her heart squeezed slightly. Shifting her gaze to the window, she willed her heartbeat to slow. "Just tell me why you're here."

"Cindy—" At that name, her body jerked and her eyes darted back to his. He heard her gasp and rushed to say, "She's fine…fine…well, as fine as she can be. Sorry, I didn't mean to scare you." His hands twisted together and he shook his head in dejection. "Jesus, I'm fucking this all up."

Seeing him so despondent, she did not want to feel sympathy, he certainly hadn't offered her any when he was berating her outside her work, but, even so, she was unable to hang on to her anger, at least not at the level she had felt before. Anger took more energy than she had left in her. "Look, Cael. Just talk to me. If nothing else, we *were* able to talk to each other so easily." Sighing, she added, "I let you come in, so I'm willing to listen. I won't bite your head off, so talk and, then, once you get out what you want to say, you can leave and it'll be over."

Cael lifted his head, eyes on Regina, his heart aching at the thought of never seeing her again. But, he knew it was her call. He fucked up and had no idea if she would forgive him.

Nodding, he said, "You're right." Still leaning forward, he relaxed his hands and allowed the words in his heart to flow. "Cindy got her wig." He watched as her eyes lit before she shuttered them again.

"Wig?" she asked, trying for ignorance, but failing.

"We know...the family knows it was you."

Regina sucked in a quick breath and it was on the tip of her tongue to refute Cael's claim. Her hand lifted involuntarily, her fingertips moving over her short hair. "How...um...how did you know? It was supposed to be anonymous."

For the first time since seeing her again, he smiled. "Oh, Red, there was no doubt. I saw the thick hair, so many colors, just like yours, and I was sure. You're the only one I know who has hair like that. It was like looking at you. I...I just knew. The sun was shining on Cindy's bed and I saw the red and gold strands all mixed together and, then, when I touched it? I knew beyond a shadow of a doubt. Tom and Kathy said they looked up the company and they will make wigs for people either from their own hair...or the hair of a friend. Hell, even Cindy said it looked like you."

She tried to look away but the light shining in his eyes held her captive. Sucking in her lips, she rubbed them together for a few seconds before finally speaking.

"I'm glad she's happy with it. I…uh…I never meant for anyone to…uh, you know…uh, know about it."

His eyes shifted to the top of her head again and he said, "Can't imagine it's much of a secret in your life. It's the kind of thing people would notice."

"Oh, yeah…well, I just…well…" She knew she was stammering but could not think of anything to say when his presence seemed to suck all her reasoning out of her.

"You can't imagine what it means to her…to the whole family. I needed to find you and let you know. Your gift was…Jesus, Red, why? Why, for a child you didn't really know?"

Swallowing, she forced her gaze to move from him, staring out the window once more. "No child should… suffer like that." She blew out a long breath, blinking furiously at the sting of unshed tears. "Every little girl should feel like a princess."

"We're all grateful…beyond grateful. There's no way to repay what you did."

She shrugged her shoulders as she stared into the distance. "Hair grows back eventually."

Silence flowed between them, not uncomfortable, settling like a heavy blanket over the room.

Finally, gaining control of her rolling emotions, she smiled a smile that did not reach her eyes, and uncurled her legs from underneath her before standing. "Well, it was nice of you to come and let me know, but it wasn't necessary…I really wanted it to be anonymous but…uh…whatever, it was nice nonetheless."

"That's not all," he blurted, halting her movements. "Please, let me continue."

Staring at him for a moment, deciding if she wanted to hear more, she eventually plopped back into her chair, too tired to keep standing. Cocking her head to the side, uncertain what else he wanted to say, she was sure of at least one thing—she did not want more of his previous censure. Looking at him now, she thought she could hear him out, let him get it off his chest, but she was wrong. She was too tired to deal with any of this. "Listen, I get that you wanted to say thanks, and I didn't want or need it, but it was kind of you all the same. And I know you wanted to apologize about…what happened…and I'm willing to put it all behind us, but you said enough last time about what you thought of me and I'm not keen to hear it again, so, if this is about you feeling bad for yelling at me, I don't need to hear it. It's done. And we're done. Now, I've got work to do—"

"I was wrong."

She stared, her heart stinging anew simply from the thought of the words he slung at her the previous time he had seen her, but the anguish on his face held her attention. "Wrong?"

"Wrong about so much." He inhaled deeply before sitting up straight and holding her gaze steadily. "What happened the night we met had never happened to me before. I'm not one to do a lot of picking up women in bars, but when I do, it's just sex. Nothing more and everyone involved knows it. But, damn, if you didn't capture me right from the beginning. I was in your presence for only ten minutes and I wanted to treat you to a night at a nice place. But it wasn't enough. Nothing with you was enough."

She tucked her legs back underneath her in a protective posture again, her heart beating quickly, uncertain she wanted to hear more. She wanted to be smart, to not fall into a trap, but with him here, now, looking and sounding so sincere, so honest, she couldn't stop herself from giving him this chance to clear the air.

"One night led to a weekend, and by the time we had a few days together, I wanted more. Not just more sex, but more of you. More of everything with you…walks, talks, laughing, eating. Fuck, I wanted to know your name. Something so simple, but it turns out it means so much. But, we'd made that stupid agreement. The problem was, I had regrets. Not in being with you, but in pretending that we weren't at the beginning of something great."

Nodding, she was not sure she wanted to respond. He was right, about all that. But with how it ended…if they were going to finish this, she needed to let him talk.

"Taking you to see Cindy that night made me feel like you were part of us. It was just instinct to have you there with me, and I'm glad you came." Taking a deep breath, he continued, "I admit, seeing everything I cared about it one room, I wondered if I had it in me to have it all…like I was being selfish by not devoting myself completely to her care and making sure she was alright." His voice got a little tense as he added, "But it turned out I didn't need to worry about that, because the next morning, you were gone."

Surprised that he was laying that at her feet, she sat up straighter, her eyes pinning his. "I…" She paused, frustration building, before clearing her throat and starting again. "I heard you that night. You thought I was sleeping, but you said you had no place in your life for more than you felt you could handle and that you needed to give everything to your family. We made no promises to each other, Cael. I thought I was doing the right thing by you. I didn't want you to feel you were letting her down by being with me. And, I don't want to be with someone who feels guilty being with me. You never know what life's going to throw at you. Your plate is full…I get that. So, I made one of the hardest decisions of my life and walked away. For you."

Cael's stomach sunk at her words. "Oh, fuck… fuckin' hell," he gasped. "I never meant to say that…shit, not where you could hear me. I was trying to think through everything…work it all out in my mind. By the morning, I knew the reality was that I wanted you and there was plenty of me to give to everyone. Sometimes we just have to work things out in our heads, you know. It doesn't mean we really feel that way."

Regina bit her lip, hearing Cael's words, but there was still one thing that couldn't be denied. "Okaaaay," she said slowly, her voice low. "I get that. I was going through some of the same emotions." She watched his square jaw tick, the muscles tight, knowing he was expecting her next question. "What I don't get, is how you went from wanting to be with me to practically calling me a cheating whore in the middle of the sidewalk, outside where I worked."

Cael's gut clenched as her words hit him like a punch to his stomach. He wanted to refute them, take them away, make them disappear. His shoulders slumped at the pain in her voice and he wondered if there was ever really a chance to make things right.

Spreading his hands to the side, he replied, "I can't take those words back, no matter how much I wish I could. Miss Ethel used to always tell me that words matter and to use them carefully." Shaking his head, he added, "Regina, I wish you could know how unlike me that was."

Lifting an eyebrow, she said, "Sure sounded like you. Pretty sure it was you standing on the sidewalk in front of me. Actually, towering over me, in fact."

"I know…you're right. But that's not what I meant. I'm someone who rarely has to apologize for what I say because I'm cautious. With you, I went against everything that is me. I used my size to intimidate, and to do that with a woman, a woman I was seeing no less, was unconscionable. My words were hateful and judgmental, and I need you to know how sorry I am."

Sighing, Regina stood and said, "You know what, Cael. It's done. I accept the thanks from your family and I hope all the best for Cindy. I even accept your apology that you didn't mean what you said…that you let your emotions spill over into anger and you said some things you now wish you hadn't. We all make mistakes. Lord knows, I have too. It's over…it's done…it's forgiven." She started toward the door, hoping he would take the hint, follow, walk through the door never to be seen again, so that she could go back to crying over him again.

She turned to usher him out but he was still sitting on the sofa, his eyes on her. Obviously, her attempt to have him leave was not working. Standing for a moment, she thought of something else that she had ignored upon the surprise of his confessions. Cocking her head to the side, she said, "How did you find me? How did you know where I live?"

Cael did not think the day could get any worse but when she learned the next truth, he was afraid it would be the last straw for her.

20

Sighing, Cael hung his head and chuckled ruefully, thinking his luck could not get any worse. Lifting his eyes, he watched the suspicion in her face as her eyes narrowed on his. Standing, he said, "Will you hear me out? Everything? Please?"

"That's what I thought I was doing earlier."

"There's more. But, I need to try to get it all out or there's no way any of this will help. It'll all just still sound so fucked up." He spread his arms out to the sofa, saying, "Please. Just give me ten more minutes."

Regina walked slowly to the other end of the sofa, once again tucking her legs up and wrapping her arms around them, curling into a protective ball, as she faced him.

He twisted his body so that he was facing her as well. "Okay…the whole thing in one, long, big, statement? I met you, wanted more than a night, spent time with you, was falling for you, got scared, and then when you left, wanted to find you. Found where you might work, took a chance, and hung out. Saw you, got excited, then saw you with another man. Figured I lost my chance, and even though it hurt, I was going to accept that. But then I noticed how close you two looked, and I figured this could not be new, which made me even more hurt, because that would mean you were with him when you were with me. Then I saw him get in a car with a woman, kiss her, and I got curious. Even angry, I cared about you and didn't want you involved with someone who might not be good for you. So, I followed him, saw him go to a home with his pregnant wife and saw their child. Went back to you and you admitted you knew about him. Everything I saw pointed to you seeing someone else while I was falling for you, and that person was married with kids, and you knew that. I was hurt that you didn't feel the same about me, and I was angry that you seemed okay with being involved with someone who had a family. That was where I totally fucked up, Red. You were right—the woman I was falling for was not that kind of woman, but I let my… my…oh, hell, my abandonment issues get in the way, and said those awful things to you."

His breath left him in a rush, but since he still had her wide-eyed attention, he sucked in another gulp of air and kept going.

"I got to thinking about it…first, I just felt sorry for myself, but then my friends began to question what I saw and I realized that even if I was right, my behavior was still completely wrong. I jumped to conclusions and didn't give you a chance to defend yourself. I knew I had to apologize, Red. There was no way I could leave things the way they were. And then, Cindy got the wig and I knew that you deserved not only my apology, but our thanks. Even if you never accept my apology, you still should have our thanks. I went to your work but they said you didn't come in anymore and wouldn't tell me how to contact you. So, uh...I went back to the house and followed the man you were with to his workplace."

Her eyebrows hit her hairline and she gasped. "You...you...?"

"I know, I know, it was crazy," he rushed. "But I was desperate." Sighing again, he continued, "I thought I was talking to the man you were involved with and I just wanted to know where you lived. Of course, he wouldn't give it out, but he knew about me. He said I broke your heart. And, that's when he told me he was your brother."

"So...you didn't just come here today because you found out he was my brother?"

"No, honest to God, you can ask him. I was there to find you so I could apologize and it was after that I found out."

She sucked in a long breath through her nose, her lips pinched together tightly. Looking down, she plucked imaginary lint off her knees, avoiding his piercing gaze.

He kept going, taking her silence as permission...or an opportunity he was not going to waste. "I saw his name and assumed your last name was his. I had already heard him call you Regina. So, it wasn't much of a search to find your address."

Her face scrunched at that last titbit of information. "Red, you need to do a better job of protecting yourself. It wasn't hard at all to find out where you lived." Deciding to press his advantage, he scooted a bit closer to her on the sofa, just enough that he could reach out and touch her fingers resting on her knees.

Not wanting to deal with the swirl of emotions churning inside, Regina chose honesty. "I don't know what to do with all this information."

His heartbeat pounding in his ears, Cael suggested. "How about take another chance on me?" Her eyes landed sharply on his and he pressed on before she could object. "We clicked, Regina. We had something special, and if we hadn't made the original agreement of no names, we might have discovered that the initial attraction that led to us wanting more time, could have ended up in our involvement. A relationship built on mutual trust. I know I fucked that up, but if you can forgive me, can you also be willing to give me...us, another chance? A real chance with real names and real possibilities?"

Sucking in her lips, Regina searched Cael's face. Part of her wanted to deny his request and send him on his way. But, as his blue eyes peered back, the longing in them speaking to the need in her, she faltered. Her gaze dropped to his hand resting on her knee, the long fingers trembling. It was odd...he was such a strong man and yet, so unsure. *I should say no. I should make him go. But we all make mistakes. We made the same one in holding to our pact when we both knew it was anything but a one-night stand, and that blew up in our faces. He has his regrets, and I have mine...*

Without realizing it, her mouth answered, "A real chance and real possibilities? That sounds like quite a leap from where we started."

His hand jerked and squeezed her knee. "All you have to do is take a leap of faith, Red. Trust what you felt with me. What we had when it was good. I didn't do that and look where we ended up. I promise you, I won't make the same mistake again."

"Walking away from you was so hard the first time, but I thought it was what you needed."

"I get that, and I'm sorry I didn't see it at the time. I was thinking out loud, which was a dumbass thing to do, and you heard it. We had just left Cindy and I was wondering how I could give you the attention I wanted to give you while giving my family the attention they needed."

"And how has that changed? We start this and you decide that it's more than you can deal with? I don't know that I can handle that again."

Cael lifted his hand and cupped Regina's face, noting it felt more fragile than he remembered. Rubbing his thumb over her cheek, he slid closer. "Baby, if we give us a chance, knowing how good it was, I know we have enough in us to make it through anything." He watched as a shadow passed through her eyes.

A sad smile curved her lips as she shook her head, "I don't know, Cael. I'm not sure either of us is strong enough to face the unknown."

"We are, Red. You've just got to take that leap of faith

with me. Please…let me prove to you that I'm in this for real."

Swallowing, Regina wanted to look away but Cael's gaze entrapped hers. *I want this. I want this so bad. But…what if…*

"I can see the *what ifs* in your eyes, but let me take them away," he begged.

Nodding slowly, she gave in to her heart's desire. Choking back a sob, she moved forward and he slid his arms around her, gathering her onto his lap.

His kiss was soft and sweet and she trembled underneath his touch. Afraid of scaring her, Cael moved his lips over hers, slow and gentle. The kiss was open mouth, wet and wonderful, but until her tongue darted out, he did not dare take it further. With the feel of her tongue on his, he angled his head, holding her cheeks in his palms, and devoured her mouth.

Moaning, Regina relaxed in Cael's hold, allowing him to guide the kiss. Her hands moved to his shoulders, the feel of his thick muscles familiar underneath her fingertips.

Without losing her lips, Cael twisted, falling back on the sofa, her body now prone on top of him. His left hand held the back of her head, the short hair silky against his fingers as his right hand roamed down her back, landing on her ass before traveling back up. She felt thinner than he remembered and guilt flew through him at the thought of her not taking care of herself after he had verbally attacked her.

Feeling the change in Cael's kiss, Regina lifted her head, her gaze searching his face. "Where'd you go?"

"Sorry, babe. I just…well, I just wondered how things have been for you since…uh, well, the last time I saw you."

Her brows lowered in confusion. "Cael, if you have a question, then I really need you to just ask it. I'm not sure what you're looking for."

"You feel a little thinner and it made me wonder if you were taking care of yourself." Cael winced, hearing the words leave his mouth, knowing they could sound like he was criticizing her appearance.

"I think I've lost a little weight, but do you seriously want to discuss that now?" She leaned back in, thrusting her tongue back inside. Hearing his groan, she continued her assault.

The feel of her breasts pressed onto his chest caused all other thoughts to fly from his mind. His hands slid under her shirt, one moving up and the other moving down underneath the waistband of her pants. Her skin was just as soft as he remembered.

She pulled away from his lips again, this time to shift up, straddling his hips with her knees digging into the sofa. Sitting astride, she whipped her shirt over her head and threw it to the floor. She had not been wearing a bra and her breasts bounced slightly with the movement. His hands moved up, cupping the mounds of rosy-tipped flesh, rolling her nipples between his fingers and thumbs.

Regina gyrated her hips, creating the friction she craved, rubbing her core over his jeans. When she was unable to take it anymore, she slid down his thighs and struggled to free one leg from her leggings and panties.

Her hand then moved to his jeans' zipper, sliding it over his thick cock. He lifted his hips and jerked his pants and boxers down just enough to free his cock.

She mounted him again, this time raised up on her knees, positioning over the tip as he fingered her clit. Settling slowly, she impaled herself on his shaft, a hiss leaving both of their lips at the contact. With her hands on his shoulders, she rocked up and down, taking him deeply.

His fingers gripped her hips, assisting as she tired. "Let go, baby," he ordered softly. "I'll take it from here."

She bent forward so her clit rubbed against his pelvis, as he thrust in and out of her hot, slick core. "Harder," she begged.

"Remember, Red. You don't ever gotta beg." He pumped harder and faster, grinning as her breathing hitched and her orgasm hit.

She felt her sex tightening, gripping his cock as the shock waves moved from her inner muscles throughout her body. Crying out, she clenched him until the last wave eased, leaving her crashing down on his chest.

With his hands still clamped around Regina's hips, Cael thrust several more times until he groaned, his muscles taut, pouring himself into her warm channel. His arms encircled her back, cradling her soft body, lying sated on his. One hand slid to her head, his fingertips encountering her shorn locks once again. The visible reminder of her selfless gift to Cindy had his fingers jerking in a spasm.

Regina felt the way Cael's hand rested on her head and knew he was thinking of her hair. Suddenly self-conscious, she buried her face in his neck, not wanting to see his expression.

Cael loved having Regina tucked underneath his chin, but he realized she was hiding more than cuddling. "Red? Baby, look at me."

She lifted her head slightly, her eyes shifting from his to his chin.

He moved his fingers along her short hair, the silky spikes soft. "You're beautiful."

Blushing, she ducked her head. "You don't have to say that—"

"Not lying," he vowed. Sliding one hand to her cheek, he lifted her chin with his thumb until her eyes were back on his. "You were always beautiful and your hair was part of that. But, more importantly, you have a beautiful soul. Inside and out. Everything about you. So, long hair or short...it doesn't matter, 'cause every inch of you is perfect."

As Regina's eyes became watery, Cael's face became fuzzy. His thumb moved from her chin to her cheek, catching a tear before it dropped.

"Don't cry, baby. Not now...not when we've moved beyond what tore us apart and found a new us."

"New us?"

Grinning, he said, "Real names and real possibilities."

Her lips curved in a soft smile and she replied, "I like that." They continued to stare into each other's eyes for a moment before she sighed heavily. "What now?" she asked, her voice timid.

"Now? We begin us."

Driving down the road, Cael reached over, linking his fingers with Regina's, resting them on her thighs. He noted the slight shaking but was unsure as to the cause. As they pulled into the hospital parking lot, he turned off the engine, but before he opened the door, he turned to her, giving her fingers a squeeze.

Her face, tight and unsmiling, had him giving a slight tug on her hand as he called her name, drawing her attention to his face. "Regina, what's wrong?"

Licking her dry lips, she shook her head. "I don't know about this, Cael." Her right hand absently lifted to her hair, her fingers giving a nervous tug on a short lock.

He shifted in his seat, reaching over to place his hand over hers. "Babe, you're not getting this, but my family is so grateful to you and Cindy just wants to see you again." Leaning in to place a soft kiss on her lips, he added, "And, you're gorgeous but, if it makes you feel better, slip your hat on to keep the chill away."

Sending a grateful smile his way, she pulled her hand from his and tugged on her knitted hat that matched her scarf. "I'm not self-conscious about my hair, but I just hate for it to be so in-your-face to your family. I truly meant for the wig to be given anonymously. It feels weird for them to know it was from me."

"I get that, but you need to see with your own eyes how your gift has made such a difference to Cindy. It's like she's come alive again. You've given her back part of herself that she lost." Kissing her again, he tugged on her hand, mumbling against her lips. "Come on, baby."

As he moved around the front of the truck, she sucked in a deep breath before letting it out slowly. Assisting her down, he wrapped an arm over her shoulders warming her from the chill wind that swept over the parking lot.

Entering the lobby, he picked up his visitor's badge and waited for hers to be made. She looked up at his face, smiling down at her, as they entered the elevator. Linking fingers, he led her down the hall to the same room they had visited together before. Washing, they donned the gowns and masks.

Stepping inside, Regina's eyes were instantly drawn to the flash of color in the bed. The reddish-blond wig on Cindy's head, combined with her smiling face, caused her feet to stumble. Glad for Cael's tight hold on her hand, she quickly righted herself, walking closer to the bed.

"Cindy-loo, look who I brought to see you today," he called out.

Kathy and Tom intercepted them before they could

reach Cindy, both pulling her out of Cael's grip and engulfing her in hugs of their own.

"Oh, my God, you have no idea how much your sacrifice means to us...to Cindy," Tom said, his eyes filled with tears.

Kathy, having lost the battle to quell her own tears, let them spill down her cheeks as she pulled her close. "Bless you, bless you. Oh, God, I don't even know your name."

"Meet Regina Nunzel," Cael introduced.

Kathy, eyes still watery, lifted her hands up to touch her short hair sticking out of her cap. "Oh, Regina."

Embarrassed, she refuted, "Please, it was no sacrifice."

"Mommy, I want to talk to her," Cindy complained loudly.

Cael gently pulled her away from his sister and led her over to the bed. She felt her breath catch in her throat as she stared at the smiling child with her hair...*my hair*. Unable to stop herself, she reached out and ran her fingers through the tresses swinging just to Cindy's shoulders. The feel of her real hair sliding through her fingers felt strangely familiar, even while it was now someone else's. She shifted her focus from the hair to Cindy's upturned face, realizing the child was staring at her. She pulled off her cap and let her short hair be seen.

Offering a tremulous smile, battling the emotions threatening to overwhelm her, she softly said, "Hey Cindy."

Cindy's wide eyes dropped from her hair to her face.

Her voice childlike and full of awe, she whispered, "Do I have your hair now?"

Nodding, she blinked furiously, but was unable to contain the tears welling in her eyes. "Yeah, baby," she managed to choke out in a shuddering whisper, "you have my hair now."

"But, how?"

She touched Cindy's nose, her smile more firmly in place, and replied, "Because that's what princesses do. They can share special gifts with other princesses. This was my turn to share."

"Will I be able to share someday?" Cindy asked, her gaze never leaving hers.

Nodding, she said, "Absolutely, sweetheart. But, do you know that you already share…with all of us. Just by being you." The two of them, bound together by circumstance, smiled at each other as everyone else in the room faded away.

Cael, blinking at the sting in his eyes, watched as the beauty he had fallen for and almost lost forever held his niece's tiny hand, the two in their own cocoon. Cindy's eyes were bright and her smile wide, glowing with happiness. A movement from the other side of the room caught his eyes and he observed as Kathy, in tears, fell into Tom's arms as he pulled his wife in for a hug.

Regina bent forward and kissed Cindy's forehead, then looked down at the book on her lap and smiled. "I'll bet you'd like your Uncle Cael to read to you, wouldn't you?"

"Yes!" Cindy shouted with enthusiasm, her gaze now landing on him. "Please?"

Stepping forward, he placed his large, warm hand on Regina's shoulder, offering a comforting squeeze and nodded. "Sure, Punkin', but how about we let Regina sit and read with us?'

"Yes!" Cindy shouted again, waving as her parents nodded their tearful thanks and left the room to get something to eat.

Regina circled the bed and settled her hip on the mattress as he sat in the chair pushed up closely. Taking the book, he looked at the title and his gaze shot back to Cindy. After reading the Velveteen Rabbit the other night, he was hesitant to read another emotional book.

"Are you sure about this one?" he asked.

"I watched the movie and it was so pretty. They talk a lot about magic. I like that...thinking that there's magic all around," Cindy exclaimed. "Mommy says when I get better, we can visit a secret garden too."

Nodding, he said, "Okay, bug. Lay down and we'll start." Sucking in a deep breath, he began the abridged version of The Secret Garden.

"'Of course there must be lots of Magic in the world,' he said wisely one day, 'but people don't know what it is like or how to make it. Perhaps the beginning is just to say nice things are going to happen until you make them happen.'"

Cindy's eyes, still open after thirty minutes of reading, were lit with excitement. Her smile beamed and he reached out, placing his large hand on her thin leg, seeing her hand being held by Regina's.

"Sometimes since I've been in the garden I've looked up through the trees at the sky and I have had

a strange feeling of being happy as if something was pushing and drawing in my chest and making me breathe fast. Magic is always pushing and drawing and making things out of nothing. Everything is made out of magic, leaves and trees, flowers and birds, badgers and foxes and squirrels and people. So it must be all around us. In this garden - in all the places."

"I hope to go to a garden like that someday," Cindy whispered, the awe evident in her voice.

"You know," Regina said, "your uncle and I went to a lovely park, filled with trees and flowers. And there was a small lake as well, with ducks paddling all around. When you get out of the hospital, how about we take you there?"

"Oh, yes!" she cried. "And we can find some magic?"

Regina nodded and he continued to read.

"I am sure there is Magic in everything, only we have not sense enough to get hold of it and make it do things."

As the story continued with Colin, the little boy who thought himself ill—who was befriended by Mary and Dickon—he began to learn that magic was everywhere and had the ability to make him well.

"'I shall live forever and ever and ever ' he cried grandly. 'I shall find out thousands and thousands of things. I shall find out about people and creatures and everything that grows - like Dickon - and I shall never stop making Magic. I'm well I'm well.'"

"Uncle Cael?" Cindy's small voice sounded. He looked up from the page into her eyes.

"Yeah baby?"

"Will that be me? Will I live forever and ever?"

His breath caught in his throat, as it did so often in Cindy's presence, and he faltered, his gaze shooting to Regina's. She offered a small smile, nodding encouragingly.

"Well, uh…none of us will live forever, sweet pea. But, we'll all live just as long as we're supposed to."

Cindy's eyes held his for a long time before she relaxed her head back to the pillow. "Then, I'll hope for the magic."

"'That is the Magic. Being alive is the Magic—being strong is the Magic. The Magic is in me—the Magic is in me.'

"He had made himself believe that he was going to get well, which was really more than half the battle."

As he finished the story, Cindy's eyes closed and her breathing slowed as sleep claimed her. He closed the book and lay it on the table near her bed, which was stacked with a number of other books. Leaning over her slumbering body, he kissed her head through the mask. Hearing a hitched breath, he looked up, twisting his head to see Regina's ravaged expression.

Standing quickly, he rounded the bed and took her hand, pulling her up, surrounding her body with his arms. She buried her face in his chest, her tears soaking his shirt. He held her with calming strokes up and down her back, soft shushing noises murmured against her hair.

"Baby, she's gonna get better," he promised. "And you've already given her the magic when you gave her your hair. She believes that she'll get well…and remember, that's more than half the battle."

She nodded, her head moving against his chest, while staying buried underneath his chin. After a moment, she lifted her head, and reached for a tissue to wipe her tears. Blowing out a big breath, she turned her wobbly smile up toward him.

Reaching up, she cupped his jaw in her hand. "You're such a good uncle. Well, actually, you're such a good man."

His face softened, "Oh, Red, if I was such a good man, why was I such a dick with you—"

She stilled his words with her fingers on his lips. "No, Cael. No going back. We both started out with an idea of wanting to keep things simple, not realizing that we were right for each other. So, no going back. We can just go on from here."

Cael's eyes closed as he dropped his chin to his chest, the sweet smile on his face searing into Regina's heart. She prayed her words were true. *Go on from here. Please God, don't let me be making a mistake. I just want normal…a life with him. Please don't let me destroy this man.*

She closed her eyes as well, her heart aching with longing. Feeling his forehead touch hers, she opened her eyes, her sight filled with all that was him. Her Titan. With his massive arms around her, she felt his strength seep deep inside and she lifted on her toes, kissing the underside of his jaw.

Hearing a noise at the door, they moved back as Kathy and Tom re-entered the room, both seemingly relaxed and smiling.

As they said goodbyes and walked out of the hospital, Cael felt Regina shiver and pulled her body closer after checking to make sure her cap was pulled securely over her hair. "Let's get you home, babe," he said, hustling her into the truck where he turned up the heat.

Once there, he walked in with her and they stood awkwardly for a moment at the kitchen counter. "Do you have to go?" she asked, uncertainty lacing her voice.

Shaking his head, he said, "Nah. Done with one job and won't start on my own till next week. I got some welcome time off." He shrugged, adding, "I'll work some on my house, but...for tonight...I got nowhere I'd rather be."

Her smile relieved his worries and as he opened his arms, she stepped into his embrace. Leaning her head way back, she whispered, "Then take me upstairs. Let's go to bed."

He bent and, scooping her into his arms, kissed her lightly. "Just show me the way, Red."

22

Waking early the next morning, Regina shifted in bed and peered over her shoulder at the softened face of the man sharing her pillow. Cael Holland was a cuddler—a serious cuddler, with one arm under her neck and the other lying around her, tucked under her breasts.

She managed to slip out from his arms without waking him and padded into the bathroom, before going downstairs to the kitchen. She loved her town-house, the older building restored with exposed brick, gleaming wooden floors, and tall windows allowing the sun to wash in. But, it was a rental. She had not wanted to put money into a home until she was sure it was where she wanted to stay and, until then, she just rented.

Putting on the kettle for her tea, she also started the coffee maker and soon the kitchen was filled with the scent of bacon frying and blueberry muffins baking. Just as she placed the baking tray onto the cooling rack, arms encircled her from behind and firm lips landed on her neck.

"Mmmm," Cael moaned, his voice vibrating against her skin. "I don't know what smells sweeter, you or those muffins."

Giggling, she squirmed. "I'm ticklish," she protested. Successfully twisting in his arms, she faced him, moving her mouth to his. Accepting his tongue into her mouth, she angled her head so that her nose was out of his way, tangling her tongue in return.

He ended the kiss way too soon, pressing his forehead against hers. "Damn, Red, baby. What a way to wake up."

She grinned before stepping out of his arms and turned back to the muffins. "I've got coffee ready," she said, indicating with a head nod where the cups were located. "I'll get this plated as soon as I scramble the eggs." Suddenly, looking up, she asked, "Do you like your eggs scrambled?"

"Yeah, baby, scrambled is great."

He poured his coffee and watched as she sipped her tea while stirring the eggs. She wore a slouchy sweatshirt over her camisole and had yoga pants on with little pink fuzzy slippers on her feet. Her hair was sticking up in various directions, but the color still glistened as the sunlight came through the window. He leaned his hip against the counter and his heart seized for a few seconds, the beauty of the moment not lost on him. He had fucked up...big...and life did not often give out second chances. The idea that Regina might be lost to him right now—*No, not going there. She's here...she's forgiven me...and now we go forward.*

Plating the food, she turned to move toward her small table. Smiling up at him, she asked, "Ready?"

Dropping a kiss on her lips again, he nodded. "Absolutely."

As they ate, he looked around appreciatively at her home. "This was a good remodeling job, babe. Quality work."

She chewed while nodding. "The owner had the entire block done and I fell in love with it when I first saw it. Robert said it would be a good place to rent while I decided what I wanted to do."

His brows lowered as his gaze swung back to hers. "Rent? You don't own?"

Shaking her head, she shrugged. "I couldn't afford a down payment for a home loan when I first got out of college. I lived with Robert and his wife until I found a job and could start paying rent." She cast her gaze toward the living room, the tall, floor-to-ceiling windows letting in light over the entire space. "I was lucky to get the end unit, so I have more windows."

He thought over what she said, then something else struck him. "What did you mean by deciding what you wanted to do?"

Finishing her breakfast, Regina leaned back in her chair, still sipping her tea. Looking at Cael, she recognized worry lines creasing his forehead. "When I got out of college, I knew I wanted to work on restoring old films, but had a choice of working in several locations. I chose here because it was where Robert was, but had no idea if my job would be continuing or sustainable."

"And now?"

Smiling, she said, "I like the work and I lead a team so I have some managerial experience as well. The money isn't phenomenal, and I've had some unexpected expenses, but I've been saving as much as I can." Her eyes clouded as she said, "I might not ever be able to afford to buy a home, but I do the best I can. I can't imagine not being where Robert, Claudia, and Robbie are, especially now that they're going to have another baby soon." Winking as she sipped, she added, "And, there's a certain Titan I would now like to see more of."

"Oh, there is, is there?" Cael asked, his worry easing as he leaned forward, capturing Regina's mouth. After a moment, he pulled back, knowing if he did not, he would carry her back upstairs to bed. Adjusting himself, he asked, "How would you like to go to my house today? I've got a little bit of work to do and I'd love to show it to you."

Smiling she nodded enthusiastically. "That would be lovely."

Standing, they placed their dishes in the dishwasher and he helped her clean the few pans in the sink. Walking arm and arm up the stairs, he tucked her close. Once finished with their shower, he said, "How about taking an overnight bag?"

"Hmmm, big boy, got some plans for me?"

Catching her around the waist, he lifted her for another kiss. "Oh, yeah. When you're with me, I've always got plans."

Eyes focused out the windshield, Regina stared at the tree-lined street of the picket-fenced neighborhood that Cael was driving through. "Wow," she breathed.

His head jerked to the side, wondering what her thoughts were. He realized in that moment how much he hoped she liked what she was seeing, but couldn't tell from her expression. "Uh…you want to define *wow*?"

She looked over, a smile of wonder on her face. "This is your neighborhood? It's not at all what I pictured." Regina watched as a nervous smile curved Cael's lips. Reaching over, she placed her hand on this thigh. "Oh, Cael, I'm just in awe. Somehow I never imagined you living in such a sweet neighborhood…a place where kids run and play and moms push strollers down the street." She looked back out the window and, shaking her head slightly, said, "This is…perfect."

Relaxing, Cael viewed the street, trying to see it through Regina's eyes. "When I started considering purchasing I knew this was the kind of neighborhood I wanted to find a house in. Whether I fixed it up and sold it or kept it for myself, I knew a house here would resell really well 'cause lots of young families would be interested. And, if I decided it was where I wanted to be, then when I met someone special, it would be the type of neighborhood I could raise a family in."

Regina's heart soared at Cael's words, but she kept that to herself. Eyes peeled toward the street, she tensed, excited, as the truck slowed down and turned into the driveway of a sweet two-story, gabled Cape

Cod house with an obvious addition being built onto the back. Several tall trees were in the front yard, each surrounded by a mulched flower bed. The flowers were long gone now that it was autumn, but it was easy to imagine them in full bloom in the summer.

The white-sided house with a grey roof sported dark green shutters and a matching green front door, nestled in a quaint front porch. A two-car garage extended from the side and the windows on the second floor extended in gables.

"I'll say it once again...wow," she grinned, taking it all in.

His heart light, Cael winked and said, "Let's go in." Rounding the hood, he opened her door and assisted her down. Fingers linked, they walked up the path to the front door. Stopping, he said, "I added the front porch when I first bought the place since I needed to re-roof the entire house anyway."

While the front porch was not huge, Regina noted the space was more than enough to hold two rocking chairs to sit and enjoy the view of neighbors walking along the street. Giving a mental shake, she chastised herself. *It's way too soon to start imagining yourself here!*

But, as soon as Cael opened the front door, her imagination took flight again. The dark oak, distressed hardwood floors were refinished and extended from the living room on the left, straight across the entry foyer to the dining room on the right. A wooden table with six chairs was centered in the dining room and a sideboard with hutch graced the back wall. As her gaze swung back to the living room, she spied a comfortable sofa and three overstuffed chairs facing the brick fire-place with a large, flat-screen TV in the corner. The mantle held several framed pictures and it was easy to see the ones of him, Cindy, Kathy, and Tom. Several others held photographs of a group of boys, then later men, all smiling, often with an older woman in their midst.

"Let me take your coat," he offered, interrupting her perusal, and after she shrugged it off, he hung it up in a small coat closet by the front door. Taking her hand, he said, "I'll give you the tour."

He pointed out the obvious living and dining rooms that she had already been perusing, then walked down the hall, past the staircase, to the kitchen.

"Here's where I've spent a lot of time," he explained. "The original floorplan included large rooms, but there was only a kitchen, powder room, dining and living room downstairs, with just two bedrooms and a bath-room upstairs. There's also a basement where the washer and dryer was located. When I first bought the house and knew I had to re-roof, I expanded the back of the house, like with the front porch, and included a back room for the laundry and mudroom. I ripped out the old vinyl flooring and gutted the kitchen straight away too."

She peered at the gleaming appliances, same hard-wood floor as in the rest of the downstairs, granite countertops, and white-painted cabinets. The room was painted a green so pale, it was almost white, exuding a calm over the entire space. "Do you cook?" she asked, looking at the large, gas stove.

Chuckling, he said, "I do all right, but I'm no gourmet chef."

She turned to stare at him, smiling so proudly in his kitchen, his large body fitting perfectly in the space. Unable to keep a grin from slipping out, she walked to him and slid her arms around his waist. "It's beautiful, Cael. And, while not what I expected, I now see it is so you."

Appreciating Regina's response to his house, Cael kissed the top of her head and said, "Let's keep exploring." He led her up the stairs and pointed out the two open doors to either side, exposing the identical-sized bedrooms, one filled with boxes and the other with a California king mattress and a dresser taking up almost all the space.

She lifted her eyebrow and he laughed. "Oh, yeah, Red. A man my size has got to have a big bed, but damned if the thing barely fits. That was one of the reasons I knew I needed a new master bedroom."

The back of the hall had a large piece of plastic hanging from floor to ceiling. Pulling it aside, he said, "Come on."

Stepping through into the new addition, Regina could see where Cael had moved the hall bathroom to the side and another open door led to what he described would be a master suite. The new master bedroom was large with windows open to the back yard. A walk-in closet and Cael-sized master bathroom was on one side, including a garden tub, separate shower, double sinks and a private toilet room. Eyes wide, she twirled in the space and said, "Now this is a room I can see you in!"

Grinning, he nodded. "Yeah, it's kind of hard for someone who's my height to live in a small house. One of the reasons I chose this one to begin with was the ten foot ceilings throughout the house. I made sure to do the same in the addition."

"It looks almost finished...how much do you still have to do?"

"The plumbing and electricity is all in. Worked on the bathrooms first...both in here and in the expanded one in the hall. I wanted the bathrooms to be functional as soon as possible." Leading her back into the master bedroom, he added, "Once the framing was up, I got my friends to help with the drywall and ceilings. It's ready for painting, which is not my favorite part, but with a sprayer, it'll go fast. Once that's done, then I can lay the wooden floors to match the other bedrooms and hall up here."

She observed the way his eyes lovingly surveyed the space and felt his pride in his home. "Beautiful," she whispered, speaking of both the house and the man in it.

He looked over, his smile still firmly in place and moved to her, kissing the top of her head. "Glad you like it, Red. That means a lot to me."

Uncertain if he simply liked her opinion or perhaps hoped she would be spending a lot of time here, she sucked in her lips and offered a slight nod as they turned to go back down the stairs. Once there, he led her through another plastic tarp into the downstairs portion of the addition.

Here, she viewed a large den, complete with another fireplace and built-in bookshelves. A bay window extended at the back with a bench underneath. She immediately imagined a thick cushion where someone could curl up with a book. French doors on the right led to a brick patio and the tree-filled back yard.

She let out a huge breath, saying, "Cael, you've taken a sweet little home and are turning it into a gorgeous house that any family would be thrilled to live in."

Regina's words warmed his heart, expressing exactly what Cael had wanted to accomplish. He remained silent, not daring to breathe the words in his mind, of how he wanted it for himself...a house that was a home...a family. *And, now, with the woman standing in front of me.*

23

Sitting at the dining room table, finishing the lunch they prepared together, Regina settled back in her chair, sipping the tea Cael had surprised her with. "Can I ask you something?"

He looked over, smiling, and replied, "Babe, I've got no secrets. Ask away."

"Can you tell me about your family? You've mentioned Miss Ethel, but now that I've met Kathy, I don't quite understand how it all worked."

Nodding, he said, "Let me clear this off and we can get comfortable."

She helped him take the plates to the sink, rinse them off, and put them in the dishwasher. He grabbed another beer and refilled her tea, taking both into the living room and placing them on the coffee table. Settling on the sofa, he took her hand in his, linking their fingers as he often did. His gaze drifted to the frames on the mantle, and a faraway smile curved his lips.

"My dad was career Army. I remember him being gone a lot, but loved it when he'd come home, grab me up and toss me in the air. He was a big man…reddish-blond hair that he gave to me and was passed down to Cindy."

She smiled, her mind filled with the image of a man, so alike in looks to Cael, tossing up a little boy, happy to be home. Suddenly the image morphed into Cael doing the same with his child. Her breath left her in a whoosh, but she quickly recovered so he would not notice. "Go on," she encouraged, her voice shaky.

Sighing, he said, "One day a military Chaplain and some others in uniform came to the house…Dad had been killed." She gasped, but he continued as she squeezed his hand. "He'd come back from his overseas tour and had been killed here on a routine training exercise when his helicopter went down."

"Oh, Cael, I am so sorry," she said, her heart now aching.

He nodded, "Yeah, me too. He was a good man and from what I remember, a good father."

"How horrible for you and Kathy, and your mom also. How old were you?"

"I was five. Kathy was a teenager…she's eight years older than me. But, Mom…well, she fell apart and never really managed to become strong for us." Cael observed the sadness in Regina's eyes, but with her nod, he continued, "Mom began taking pills and usually washed them down with alcohol. Kathy took over raising me for the next couple of years as Mom slowly killed herself."

"Is she…?"

Nodding, he said, "One day we were walking home from school and saw the ambulance and neighbors outside. Mom's death was ruled an accidental overdose. She never left a suicide note, but I often wondered if that hadn't been her goal. For her, life without Dad just wasn't worth living, which I can kind of understand now, in a way, but, gotta tell you, for a kid…that shit stings—believing that you weren't enough to keep her going, keep her happy."

"I…I can't even imagine how horrible that must have been for you." Regina's eyes filled with tears, the image in her mind once more morphing, this time to a little boy whose mother emotionally abandoned him."

"She stopped living before she stopped *living*," Cael said, his voice still carrying traces of anger that he figured would be with him forever. He watched as a tear slid down Regina's cheek and reached up to wipe it away. "Oh, baby, don't cry for me. I survived. I landed in a good place and am a better man for it."

Sucking in a breath that hitched, Regina swallowed back the sob and simply nodded, unable to speak.

"And that's when I landed with Miss Ethel. We had an elderly grandmother, our only living relative. She was able to take us in, but quickly realized that a young boy was going to be way too much for her to raise. I was eight, growing like a weed, and Kathy was already sixteen, had a part-time job after school and would be able to help out."

"So, you two were split."

"Yeah," he sighed again. "It totally sucked, but was

really for the best. I knew Granny loved me, but she was right. I wouldn't have had the best life with a woman who had health issues and wouldn't have been able to do much with a little boy. So, I went into the system, but landed with Miss Ethel, known as the best foster mom around." Shrugging, he smiled, and said, "So, it all ended well. I didn't get to see Kathy too much for a couple of years, just because it was hard on Granny. But, Miss Ethel had us keep in contact and, as you can see, we're very close."

Leaning against his shoulder, she settled back into the cushions to be able to see his face well. "Tell me about her."

Cael grinned, the memories slamming into him. "She took in little boys and, somehow, turned us into men. Good men."

He also settled back, his eyes moving to the framed picture on his mantle. "She was a widow with a large house to share, a heart full of love to give, and the patience of a saint. When I got there, I was her fifth child that stayed long term. There were others who came also and stayed, then a few came and went…more emergency placements. When I got there, Zander, Rafe, Jayden, and Jaxon were there. Zander was a year older than me and the twins were a year younger. She raised her boys to be brothers and we still are today. Zeke came along a lot later, but he's just like a brother too."

"That's amazing," she said, her gaze on his face, now softened with the memories.

"Yeah, it is. In fact, they're the ones helping me build the addition. She raised us to know what family is truly about and those lessons stuck." He watched as her lips curved and a small smile lit her face. Leaning over, he placed a sweet kiss on those lips before wrapping his arm around her, pulling her close to him again.

They sat quietly then, the peace of the moment sliding over them, before he said, "I want you to meet them. Meet all of them, including Miss Ethel."

She hesitated for only few seconds before agreeing, "I'd be honored."

"Can I ask about you? I mean, I've now met your brother, although it was under less than optimal circumstances. What about your family?"

"Mine is...strange. I mean, not like yours, but not really picture-perfect either." Regina felt Cael's body shift and, once more, found herself close while facing him. Giggling, she said, "You need to see me for this?"

Nodding, he said, "Yeah, Red. Anytime you're laying something heavy on me, I want to see your face. I want to be able to see what's passing through your eyes, whether it's joy or sadness. I want to see it, read it, and know how to take it in."

She blinked, surprised, but, honestly, that was one of the sweetest things she had ever heard. Someone wanting to take all she had to give and to know what to do with it without her having to say anything. *Well, all I'm willing to share.*

Licking her lips, she said, "My story is kind of the opposite. Your mother couldn't live without your dad and my mother couldn't live with mine."

"Oh, damn," he said, his thumb gently rubbing her hand.

"Yeah…kind of the classic anti-love story. Mom and Dad met in college. She supposedly hated her parents and really wanted to escape from under their thumb, so, they got married right away. She wanted a man who would take care of her so she didn't work, putting all that on Dad. She got pregnant with my brother right after they graduated and then they had me about three years later. Things just got worse and worse. Maybe her staying at home would have been okay if she had been there as a mom for us but, quite frankly, she wasn't very maternal. Dad worked all day long and then would come home to children who needed someone. Considering she also didn't cook, he usually made dinner too."

Shifting slightly, she held his gaze as she continued, "I was about ten years old when some…um…things happened and she decided that she had had enough of playing mom. Dad finally refused to bend to her wishes because his attention was focused on…uh…, well, me and my brother. Within a year she decided she was done with our needs. By that, I mean, she found another man that made more than Dad did, had no children, and offered her a chance to live in a big house with maid service and a cook. For Dad, it meant he didn't have to pay a dime of alimony and, believe me, we haven't heard from her since she left. Thank God, for us, she moved to another state."

"Bet that shit stung just like my mom—checking out on her family," Cael stated, not asking, because he knew without her answering that that kind of response from a parent did sting. And it left a mark.

Nodding slowly, she agreed. "Yeah. It stung. I…well,

all of us, went through a lot and my own mom not really caring was hard. My dad was great, though. He took care of us, making the best of a bad situation. He was wonderful with a budding teenage girl and, honestly, after watching my mom, her doing what she did, I didn't want to be anything like her. I kept my adolescent hormones in check—no bitchiness, no PMS, no smart mouth. Both Robert and I pitched in to help around the house. We three became like the three musketeers. And you know what?" she asked, her eyes sparking with light. "We realized we always had been *'we three'*, even when Mom had been around. Now, we just didn't have to pretend."

"So, life got better."

"Absolutely. No doubt. Looking back, I know it must have killed Dad to have his wife, the mother of his children, walk out on us, especially when she did, but honest to God, Cael, life was so much better. Easier. Calmer. Happier. I saw Dad smile more in those years than I did the whole time she was with us." A faraway expression crossed her face, and she added, "He always said Robert and I made his life worth living and that we were the joy of his existence." She lifted her gaze to his and asked, "Isn't that the most wonderful thing a parent can say to a child? That they are the joy of their existence?"

"Absolutely, Red. He was right. And now? He still in the area?" As soon as the words left his mouth, he knew the answer, a cloud of sadness passing through her eyes again. Immediately cupping his hands on her cheeks, he whispered, "Oh, baby."

Regina swallowed back the lump in her throat and shook her head. "No...Dad died two years ago from a heart attack. He always took such good care of himself, but the doctors said it was probably congenital and he never knew it."

"So, it's just you and Robert?"

Nodding, her face softened again as a smile curved her lips. "He's always been a great big brother and still is. His wife is a sweetie and their little boy is a dear. And, as you've seen, I'm going to become an aunt again."

At that reminder, Cael grimaced, but Regina immediately grabbed his cheeks and held him close. "No...no regrets. We both made mistakes, remember? You told me we were moving on."

Smiling, he leaned forward the inch it took to capture her lips. As the heat rose from the melding of their mouths, he swooped her up, stalking upstairs to his California king bed on the floor, anxious for the time when he could have her in the new master bedroom...permanently.

"Most romantic movie?"

"Casablanca," Regina said, with no hesitation, staring at the rock-hard abs in front of her face as Cael lay against the pillows piled up next to the wall.

The sheet was barely covering her ass as she lay on her stomach by his side. Cael's attention was riveted on the long expanse of her back, his gaze...and hand, trailing along the delicate curves and soft skin.

"No kidding?" he asked.

"According to the American Film Institute, Casablanca is considered the number one greatest love story of all time." She grinned up at him, adding, "And, is the most quoted."

"I would have guessed Gone with the Wind."

"It's the second greatest love story of all time."

Laughing, he asked, "Are you a walking encyclopedia of movies?"

She clutched the sheet to cover her breasts as she rolled over, giggling as he frowned. "My dad loved old movies. We would watch them all the time and he would regale us with all sorts of trivia about the actors, quotes, awards. You name it, he knew it."

"Sounds nice, babe," Cael said, loving the smile on Regina's face as she reminisced about her dad.

"It was," she enthused. "All my friends would be at the theater watching the latest chick-flick and I was spending Friday nights at home with Dad and Robert, watching old movies."

"I bet I've watched a lot of the oldies myself. Miss Ethel wanted to make sure we boys were exposed to classics, both movies and books."

"She sounds marvelous."

They lay quiet for a few minutes, well sated from earlier sex, letting the evening shadows slowly move across the bed on the floor.

"Would you like to meet her soon?"

Smiling, she looked up into his face, biting her lip. "I...I guess so. Do you think she would—"

He interrupted her, bending over to kiss her words

away. "She'd be pissed if I didn't bring you around to meet everyone."

"Then, I'd be honored," she said, letting a yawn slip from her lips, barely keeping her eyes open.

"You okay? You seem really tired."

"You must have worn me out," she joked, as her eyes closed.

He kissed her forehead and slid down further, pulling her already sleeping body close.

24

Cael pulled up outside Regina's townhouse and parked his truck. Turning toward her, he leaned over, kissing her until she breathlessly pulled back.

"Stop," she protested weakly. "If we keep kissing, I'll invite you in, we'll end up in my bed, and you won't get to work and I'll get no work done."

"Sounds like a plan."

They held each other's gazes for a moment, lost in each other's eyes, until finally, blinking, she shook her head. "I'll see you later?"

"Yeah. I'll call first. I'm meeting with the attorneys and Terrance today to sign the partnership papers so that next week we can start taking over contracts."

"Good luck," she whispered against his lips, capturing them one more time. After a long, wet kiss, she allowed him to get out and assist her down from his truck.

He kissed her head, climbed back in and pulled back out into traffic.

Turning, she opened her door, jumping as a hand rested on her arm. Blinking, she saw Robert standing on her bottom step.

"Oh, you scared me. Have you been waiting long?"

He wasted no time, immediately asking, "Do you know what you're doing?"

Pulling back, she narrowed her eyes and said, "Seriously? I'm not some sixteen-year old who needs her dad to question her choice of dates."

"That's not what I'm doing here, Regina. Come on... think about it. Do you know what you're doing?"

Shoulders slumping, she said, "Come on in and I'll put on some coffee and fix some tea." She led him into the kitchen, where she fixed their drinks before watching him sit down on the stool at the counter. Facing him, she leaned on her elbows, her teacup in her hands.

"I'm just worried, sis. You've got a lot going on and you look like you haven't slept in days."

Nodding slowly, she said, "I know you're worried, Robert. And, I know with Dad gone, you feel like it's up to you to take care of me—"

"If I don't, who will?" he snapped. Her face fell and he immediately apologized. "Oh, fuck, I'm sorry. That didn't come out the way I meant." He reached across the counter and placed his hand over hers. "I want to be here for you. So does Claudia. We're family and always will be. But, this guy—"

"Cael. His name is Cael."

"Okay, Cael. Are you seeing him now? The no names and no regrets guy?"

"Yes, but remember, that idea was as much mine as it was his. In fact, to be honest, it was more my idea."

"So, what's changed? If it was your idea, why get with him now?"

"Because what we feel is real." Seeing the doubt in her brother's eyes, she said, "I didn't question your motives when you got with Claudia, so why are you questioning mine?"

He pinched his lips and held her gaze until his eyes finally dropped to his cup. "Dammit, Regina. This isn't the same."

They remained quiet for a moment, the silence broken only by the ticking of the clock on the wall.

Blinking away tears, she whispered, "I just want something as normal as love. To be loved. Feel love. Is that so wrong?"

He rounded the counter and enveloped her in his arms. She rested her head on his shoulder and closed her eyes, imagining her father's arms around her, as another tear fell.

"I just want you happy and healthy and to have everything your heart desires," he said, mumbling into her hair.

"I know...me too." Sighing heavily, she said, "But nothing in life is certain."

"If he's the guy for you...and you're sure that the time is right, for all the reasons why it might be wrong...then I'm all for it, sis." He hesitated before adding, "And I'm sorry I didn't let you know that he came to see me...I meant to, I really did, but...I was worried for you, too."

Looking into his face, she read his grimace, knowing that he was worried she'd be angry with him.

"I know he did, he told me, and I understand why you didn't. I'm not mad at you for that, in fact, I love you for it. You're a great big brother. And I have no idea if the time is right," she admitted, pulling away to stare into his eyes. "But I can pray it is."

Nodding, he kissed her forehead. "That's all any of us can do, sis."

Cael took the loaded picnic basket out of his truck and linked fingers with Regina. Walking toward the lake in the park, he was glad for the warm, sunny autumn day. Glancing to the side as they walked, he saw the wide smile on her face as she scoped out the perfect spot for their picnic. Once decided, she spread the blanket on the ground and sat down looking up expectantly.

Grinning, he plopped down beside her, offering a kiss before setting the basket on the blanket and opening the top. "Gotta admit, I'm famished."

"Well, good, 'cause I fixed a lot." She quickly looked over at him and amended, "Although it's not fancy. I hope that's alright?"

"Absolutely," he assured. "Simple picnic food is perfect."

She pulled out large sandwiches, made from hoagie rolls and filled with deli-sliced turkey, ham, and roast beef, along with lettuce, tomatoes, onions, and pickles.

"Damn, Red. These look good," he said, taking a bite.

She added potato chips, deviled eggs, and fruit salad to the fare and they sat quietly as they ate, both watching the ducks on the lake.

After finishing the pieces of cherry pie she included, he leaned back, his upper body resting on his arms bent behind him, and she snuggled up next to him.

"You still feel like one of those ducks?" he asked, merriment in his voice.

Her quietness surprised him and just as he was about to question her further, she replied softly, "Yeah. I think perhaps I'm more like the ducks now than I've ever been. Calm on the surface but paddling like crazy underneath."

Something about her words concerned him, but as she twisted around, her body lying half on his, her beautiful face turned up toward his, all other thoughts flew from his mind and he said the only thing left. "I love you."

The air grew still around them, as though the world had stopped on its axis, as he waited for her response.

Regina's breath caught in her throat as she stared into Cael's eyes, shining with the truth of his confession. Her lips curved ever so slightly as she replied, "I love you, too."

He rolled in a swift movement, putting her underneath his massive body, his weight held on his forearms planted on the blanket. Cupping her face in his hands, he kissed her...light and sweet, the taste of wine and cherries intoxicating.

She wrapped her arms around his back, holding him tight. She loved the feeling of his body surrounding hers...*as though nothing bad could ever touch me if he were near.*

Lifting his head, Cael rolled off to the side while trying to keep his cock from straining his jeans, aware of their public surrounding. This moment was too important to be reduced to a sexual feeling. He brushed Regina's lips again with his, murmuring, "I love you, Regina. Now and always."

"Always is a long time," she said, her eyes searching his.

"And that's how long my love will last."

Nodding slowly, Regina kissed Cael in return, wedding vows ringing in her ears. *Until death do we part.*

Cael and Terrance walked out of the attorney's office with Terrance's uncle, and stood on the street, shaking hands.

"Boys, for many years I loved doing home restorations, but it does me good to be able to start my retirement knowing my customers will keep getting the same service that I provided."

With hugs, he walked to his truck and drove away leaving Cael and Terrance smiling at each other.

"Well, all right, partner," Terrance said. "Looks like we'll start next week on the Martin's house over on Calhoun Street."

With a grin, Cael walked away, his heart light,

anxious to call Regina. Just as he pulled out his phone, he had another idea. Instead of calling her, he placed a few other calls first.

Walking up to the house with the sweet front porch and neat yard, Regina squeezed Cael's hand in nervousness. "I can't believe you're taking me to meet Miss Ethel so soon."

"No time like the present," he replied. Stopping, he tugged on her hand slightly and she turned to look up into his face. "Listen, I need to let you know something else."

Before he could finish, they heard the screen door open and she looked up to see a tall, thin older woman step onto the porch, her white hair pulled back into a bun and her grey eyes peering at them through wire-rimmed glasses. A wide smile was on her face as she held her arms out wide.

"Welcome, child. Welcome."

Cael hurried up the stairs, escorting her up with him, introducing her to Miss Ethel. As he bent to hug his foster mom, Regina held back a smile at seeing her Titan surrounding the older woman completely, his body engulfing her in the hug. Letting her go, he stepped back to allow the women a chance to embrace.

Miss Ethel pulled her into a hug as well, her hand patting her back as she said, "My dear, I've been longing to meet you."

Stepping back, but with her hands still firmly in

Miss Ethel's grip, she replied, "Thank you, Miss Ethel. I'm very honored to meet you as well."

"Come in, come in. There's a bit of a chill in the wind today."

As they walked into the house she looked around in unabashed curiosity, longing to see where Cael had spent most of his childhood years. The living room was homey, furnished with a dark green sofa and colorful throw pillows against the back. A rug covered the center of the wooden floor and two, deep cushioned chairs sat facing the sofa. The wall surrounding the fireplace held built-in bookshelves. She could easily imagine Cael sitting there as a child reading to his heart's content.

When she caught sight of the mantle over the fire-place, it grabbed her complete attention and her feet automatically took her there. Framed photographs of little boys laughing with their arms around each other, from childhood to teenage years, filled the space. She was able to pick out Cael easily, with his height and light-colored hair. A smile spread across her face as she stared into his friendly one.

Suddenly aware of a presence next to her, she startled as Miss Ethel appeared, perusing the photographs as well.

"All my boys are so handsome," she stated, matter-of-factly. "All good. All smart. All loved."

Regina turned to her, saying, "I think a lot of their goodness can be attributed to you, Miss Ethel. Cael has told me so much about you."

"Oh, my dear," Miss Ethel said, turning to peer closely into her eyes, "I think all of us have the capacity to love those around us. And to give of ourselves to those less fortunate." Her eyes drifted to Regina's short hair and without making a fuss, she said, "Thank you."

Shrugging, her gaze unable to leave the knowing eyes staring at her, as though she knew all her secrets, Regina replied in a whisper, "It was only hair."

Leaning forward, Miss Ethel continued to hold her gaze for a moment before whispering back, "I think we both know it was a lot more than just hair for a little girl."

Her breath caught in her throat, overwhelmed with the scrutiny—and accuracy with which she was being viewed. Heat suffused her cheeks, causing a trickle of sweat to bead on her forehead. Before she had a chance to speak, Miss Ethel added, "Just remember, dear child, you will reap what you sow."

In a startling change of demeanor, Miss Ethel suddenly cried out, "Oh, my roast. Y'all come into the kitchen and, Cael, pull the roast out for me." Miss Ethel led the way toward the kitchen with Cael in tow, Regina following more slowly.

Entering the kitchen, she stood back and watched Cael pull out a huge roast from the oven. Turning, she glanced at the table in the dining room, seeing it filled with plates.

"Cael?" she said, softly, gaining his attention.

He caught the direction of her gaze, but before he had a chance to reply, they heard the roar of motorcycles coming to a halt on the street outside the house. Walking toward the front door, she observed two SUVs parking nearby. Her mouth opened, but any words were drowned out as a pickup came down the road as well.

"Sorry, babe," he said, coming up next to her and taking in her bewildered expression as she stared at the various people all starting to walk toward them. "I thought I'd have time to tell you that the whole gang is coming over." She shifted her gaze to his, still no words coming. "Honest to God, Red, they're dying to meet you."

Inhaling a deep breath, she nodded, lifting her hand to her hair. He recognized the self-conscious motion and stilled her hand as he bent to place a sweet kiss on her lips. "I've got you, baby."

Before she had a chance to respond, they were engulfed in introductions and hugs. For a moment, she was blinded by the hot-guy overload. She tried to keep the names straight, but immediately had the twins confused. She was glad to see two women approaching, as well, meeting Rosalie, who was with Zander, and Eleanor, with Rafe. Asher rounded out the group.

As everyone swept into the house, Cael made sure to keep her tucked close. Bending, he whispered, "Are you okay? I swear, if this is too much, we can leave."

She cocked her eyebrow at him and he rushed, "In my mind, we had time to talk to Miss Ethel first and the others would arrive a few at a time." Looking at the loud, noisy gathering making their way toward the kitchen, he said, "I saw this happening so differently."

A giggle erupted from her lips at his blank expression and she lifted on her toes and stopped him with a kiss. "I find most things go differently than we think."

Adjusted to the change of events, they followed everyone into the kitchen, where the others had brought the vegetables, salads, breads, and desserts. They soon settled around the large table, with the addition of a smaller table added to the end, that miraculously held them all.

After a few minutes of chatter, Asher turned to Cael. "How's Cindy?"

"She's doing okay, so far. She'll finish chemo this next week and they hope she can go home soon."

Regina smiled at Cael as he talked about his niece, then glanced around the table noting several pairs of eyes on her short hair. She felt her smile wobble as her hand reached up to finger through the back.

"Babe."

She jerked her eyes up, seeing Cael's concerned expression, and her smile strengthened. Gazing out at the others, she said with a smile, "It's okay."

Smiles greeted her in return and the conversation returned to its boisterous level. She observed the easy camaraderie among the men and the way Rosalie and Eleanor blended in just as seamlessly. At first she thought it was just the sight that was warming her, but suddenly the room felt too hot and a slight dizziness hit her. As Miss Ethel pushed her chair back, announcing dessert, Regina hopped up, glad for the excuse to escape the overcrowded room for a moment. "I'll help."

Moving around the chairs, she began to panic as the dizziness increased. Her vision grew black and she reached her hands out to grab the wall, but they only managed to break her fall as she passed out onto the floor. The last thing she heard was Cael's voice, breaking through the cacophony of other voices, yelling, "Babe? Babe!"

25

Cael prowled the ER, his brothers at his side. "What's going on back there?" he groused, staring at the door leading to the examining rooms.

Jaxon walked over, placing his hand on his shoulder. "Be cool, man. You know they're gonna check her out." He worked as an EMT and had taken care of her until the ambulance arrived.

They looked over as Rafe walked in, carrying a tray of coffee from a neighborhood coffee shop, with Eleanor accompanying him with a bag full of sugar and sweetener packets and little containers of creamers. "I hate hospital coffee," she explained, handing them out to everyone.

"Do you know anything yet?" Rafe asked.

Dragging his hand through his hair, he said, "No. They kept asking about her medical history, but I don't know anything. I called her brother and he's on his way."

Miss Ethel rose from her chair and walked quietly across the room until she stood toe to toe with him, her head tilted as she peered intently into his eyes. Lifting her hand, she placed it on his arm and said, "How strong are you, boy?"

His brow furrowed as he fought to understand her meaning. "Strong?"

Nodding, she said, "Do you love her?"

"Yes," he replied instantly.

"Do you love her with a strength that is unbounded?"

A cold trickle of fear slid over him and for a second he allowed his gaze to shoot over his brothers, seeing their expressions of confusion, before dropping back to the woman whose respect he wanted to hold more than anyone's. "I have that strength, Miss Ethel."

She held his gaze in silence for what seemed an eternity, before giving his arm a squeeze. "Good. You'll need that. For her. And for you."

Before he had a chance to question her further, the doors opened and Robert rushed in.

"Where's Regina?" he shouted, drawing the attention of everyone. His gaze scanned the room, landing on Cael and he stalked straight to him. "What the hell happened?"

"Easy, Robert. They're running tests now. She passed out—"

"I knew it. I knew this...you...were a fucking mistake. Jesus, I told her...I warned her."

Cael was struck frozen at the accusation, mouth open but unable to speak. Taking this in, Jayden stepped forward, demanding, "What are you talking about? We all saw her...it only takes one look to see she's happy with him."

Hands on his hips, Robert glared. "Fuck happy, right now," he stated firmly, startling the entire gathering. "I just want her alive."

"What...what...?" Cael finally muttered.

"She's a childhood cancer survivor, man," Robert bit out. "And it's fucking returned."

The nurse called for Robert to go back and, without hesitation, he headed through the doors, leaving Cael, stunned, standing in his wake, the others as speechless as he.

Cael stood in the doorway, his feet rooted to the gleaming tile floor, a sense of déjà vu descending. The many times he stood in the doorway, girding himself, before walking into Cindy's room came slamming back into him. Only this time it was different. It was Regina's room. *My Red. My Red has cancer.*

Hearing voices, he hesitated behind the partially closed curtain near the door that protected the patient's privacy.

"Please don't be mad," Regina was saying. "I knew I was feeling woozy, but so wanted to go meet Cael's family."

"Sis, I'm not mad. I'm worried. You've been ignoring the signs, even though the doctors told you months ago that things were getting worse."

"I know," she replied, her voice laced with regret.

"Jesus, Regina. You were going to cut your hair for *you*. That was supposed to be for *your* wig when the chemo starts again. Fuck, sis…you gave it to his niece."

Cael's legs threatened to give out from underneath him and he grabbed onto the doorframe to hold himself up. *She cut her hair for* her. *The wig was supposed to be for her. But, she gave it to Cindy.*

Regina and Robert were silent for a few minutes before she spoke again. "Is he here?"

"I think he's outside somewhere."

"Can you find him? See if he'll come in to see me. I want…no, I need to talk to him."

Cael stepped back quickly, moving to the side of the door, and waited. Robert stepped into the hall and his gaze swept around, landing on him.

"She's awake and would like to see you."

Nodding, he started back toward the door, but a hand on his arm stopped him.

"Please," Robert begged. "Be gentle with her—"

Interrupting, he said, "I know you don't know me, so I'll allow this for now. But what you gotta get is I'm in love with your sister. I'm not going anywhere." Shaking off his hand, he moved past the curtain and into the room.

Once inside, his feet took him to the bedside, but he was surprised he did not stumble along the way. Regina lay in the bed, pale with dark circles underneath her eyes, familiar machines whirring in the background.

"Hey," he said, moving to the chair and sitting before taking her hand.

Regina watched Cael enter, her eyes never leaving his face, and recognized the pain etched in his eyes. *He's just been through this with Cindy...it's too much to ask him to go through it again.*

"Hey," she replied, sighing heavily. "I'm so sorry—"

"You've got nothing to be sorry for, sweetheart."

Nodding, she countered, "Yes, I do, Cael. I've known. I've known for a while that the cancer was coming back."

He remained silent, so she forged ahead. "That night we met? I had found out that week that the tests were showing the cancer had returned. I went out that night and just wanted to have a good time. I wanted to have a drink, dance, and if I met someone, then that was fine too."

"No names," he said softly, his thumb rubbing her hand.

With a rueful snort, she agreed. "Yeah...but I had no idea how many regrets that night would bring."

"I have no regrets," he said, his voice hoarse.

Squeezing his hand, she rectified, "Oh, no regrets about you, Cael. Just regrets that I wasn't honest with you from the beginning. But, once again, I just wanted something normal. Something fun. I never counted on falling for you. So, yes...I have regrets."

"Why didn't you say anything?"

"Because we weren't supposed to become anything. And then, you took me to meet Cindy and I knew your life was full of your own family, your own needs. It seemed so selfish to add to them. God," she cried, "then you walked back into my life and I wanted you so badly,

I selfishly couldn't say no. I'm so sorry, Cael. I'm so sorry to let you get so deep with me when I...when I might..."

"No," he said, firmly. "You have nothing to be sorry for. From the moment I saw you it was already too late, Red. You were it for me. It just took me some time to realize that. And as for the other thing? You fight. *We* fight. You can beat it. You're strong."

Cael watched as a tear slid down Regina's cheek and leaned over to capture it with his thumb. They were silent for a few minutes before he asked, "What now? What will they do?"

"I know Robert told you that I had cancer as a child. I had chemo when I was eleven and went into remission." Her hand drifted up to absentmindedly tug on her hair while she added, "I lost my hair, so when it grew back, I only got it trimmed after that and kept it long. I think it was kind of like a security blanket."

Unable to hide it from her, he blurted, "I know you cut your hair for your own wig but you gave it to Cindy instead."

Eyes wide, she gasped. "You...you heard?" Her face contorted in a grimace. "I never meant for you to hear that."

"Why? Why would you do that?"

Regina stared down at her hands for a few minutes, her chin quivering as she fought to control the sob that desperately wanted to erupt. Finally, blowing out a breath, she said, "I'm an adult. I don't need that security anymore. But Cindy's just a child. And I remember how much it made me sad to lose my hair." Shrugging her thin shoulders, she added, "Honestly, it wasn't a sacrifice. I had something that I could offer. Mine will grow back and so will hers."

Cael's mind whirled with the implications of all that had happened in the past twenty-four hours. Attempting to infuse his voice with confidence he did not feel, he said, "Okay. Okay, so next steps. What is the protocol?"

Blowing out another cleansing breath, Regina forced her response to be clinical. "We caught it early and the prognosis is good, actually. Um...they'll start me on aggressive chemo and then try to find a stem cell donor. That will be the best chance to fight this once and for all."

"Try to find?"

"Familial is best, but, well, Robert isn't a good match. And I refuse to consider my nephew, Robbie, to even be tested."

"Are they the only ones?"

"Oh, no. Anyone can be a donor, as long as the match is good." Shrugging, she said, "They'll find someone. Sometimes, it can come from another person who isn't a good match for their relative, but might be a good match for me."

Cael's heart clenched inside his chest at the thought of Regina having to start the treatment. "Okay," he said. She tilted her head in silent question so he added, "Okay, well, I need to talk to the doctors and to Robert."

"I don't understand."

"I need to find out if this is the best hospital. Do you

have the best doctors? Are you getting the best treatment? Are you—"

"Whoa..." she said, a slight smile creeping out for the first time since he entered the room. "Don't get ahead of yourself. I've got everything under control. I've got my oncology team in place, so I'm good."

"Good? You call passing out and having to be rushed to the hospital good?"

"Cael, shhh. Yes, granted, this has pushed forward the treatment that I hoped I might be able to avoid, but it's under control."

He quieted, but his mind continued to race. *Cancer. Chemo. Stem cell transplant.* Two doctors entered the room, interrupting his thoughts. He wanted to stay to listen to what they had to say, but they asked for privacy as they examined Regina. Nodding, he bent over to kiss her forehead. "I'll be back," he promised.

"She needs her rest," Robert curtly stated, walking into the room.

Turning to him, he growled, "I'm not going to keep her from resting, but I'll be back."

"Gentlemen, what she needs is a calm environment, not being exposed to arguing," one of the nurses, who walked in after Robert, proclaimed.

Cael held Regina's gaze and squeezed her hand. "I need to go talk to the others."

"They're out there?" she asked with surprise. "Please tell them to go home and make sure Miss Ethel gets home as well." Her face softened. "Honestly...I'll be fine."

Squeezing her hand one last time, he walked out of

the room toward the waiting area, his heart pounding with the desperate out-of-control feeling he felt so often with Cindy. For a split second, he wondered if he were strong enough to do it again.

That evening, Cael returned to Regina's room. Entering, he was grateful to find Robert gone. He did not blame her brother for his protectiveness, but he really wanted time alone with her. Slipping inside, he found the lights turned down low, her still form underneath the covers.

Tiptoeing over, he observed her sleeping, so he sat down in the chair next to her bed and stared, his mind still churning over the events of the day.

"Oh, Red," he whispered, his gaze drifting over her short hair, knowing now why she cut had it so much shorter than what was needed for the wig. Soon, even the short hair would be gone. And the weight loss would get worse. And the nausea. And the fear. And everything else that goes along with the diagnosis and treatment.

"I'd give anything if you didn't have to face this. Anything if we'd had more time before we were dealt this hand." He rested his forearms on the bedrail and lowered his head to his arms, fear threatening to choke him. "God, baby, you gotta know how badly I wish you to be well." He lost track of time, sitting by her side, before he finally pushed up, out of the chair, and stood over her bed. Bending to kiss her forehead once again, he whispered, "I want nothing but the best for you, Red. Goodbye, baby."

He turned and tiptoed back out of the room.

Lying in the bed, not sleeping, Regina felt a tear slide down her cheek.

26

The shaft of sunlight slid through the window, but Cael did not feel the warmth. He sat, his elbows resting on his knees, his head in his hands.

He lifted his head, his eyes red-rimmed, and peered around the room at his brothers. "She gave her hair to Cindy. The same hair that was originally supposed to be for her own wig." Swallowing hard, he asked, "Who does that? Who makes that kind of sacrifice in the face of their own need?"

"Someone who knows what it's like to lose," Miss Ethel replied, capturing the other's attention. "She lived through this once and knows she can beat it again. And, she knew that for a child, the gift of hair gave her the courage to work on beating it also."

Wiping his eyes, he said, "I don't know what to do. I want to make things better but have no idea how."

Zander spoke, his voice soft and low. "Did she say why her brother can't be a donor?"

"Something about him having a health risk."

"So, what can they do?" Jayden asked.

"They've got donors and can work to find a close match. Supposedly it's easier to find a stem cell match than when they used to do bone marrow transplants."

"And the chemo?"

"High doses before they do the stem cell transplant. She'll stay in the hospital during it all." Scrubbing his hand over his face, he said, "I went by this evening but she was asleep."

Miss Ethel's knitting lay still at her feet as she leaned forward, her hand outstretched clutching onto his arm. "You're hurtin', son, but you'll power through and come out stronger."

"What if I don't?" his broken voice asked. "What if I'm not strong enough?"

"You know, I've always said that God doesn't give us more than we can bear, but Cael, that doesn't mean He expects us to bear it alone. When it becomes over-whelming, that's when we hand it back to Him. Let Him carry it and carry us as well." She held his gaze, adding, "You'll know what to do. And, when you decide, God'll carry you through…with the help of all of us, as well. That's what family is, son. What family does."

"Fuck, Regina…this sucks," Robert said, talking to her on the phone. "Robbie's got a cold and your doctors said that since he had a fever and I've been exposed, I can't come to the hospital right now."

"It's okay," she assured, although her heart was not

really agreeing with her statement. "Please tell him I hope he feels better."

"I should be able to come back to see you within two days, assuming his cold goes away."

"It's fine. They'll start my chemo tomorrow and I'll have intense dosages for the next week, then they'll get a match for the stem cell."

His voice caught, as he said, "Sis, I'm so fuckin' sorry. Hopefully, Cael will show up and can spend some time with you."

Blinking back the tears, more at hearing her brother's agony than her own, she said, "Probably not. I mean, he's got work to do."

"Is there something you're not telling me?"

"No, of course not, Robert. I just think that now's not the right time to focus on anything but my health."

Silence moved through the airwaves as she twisted a thread in the blanket. Unable to take it any longer, she said, "I'll talk to you tomorrow, okay?"

After goodbyes and disconnecting, she held on to the phone and whispered into the dark room, "I just don't think that a happily ever after is going to happen for all of us."

Sitting in her hospital bed the next morning, Regina tried to tamp down the fear over her upcoming chemo treatment. A noise at her door had her looking up, stunned when Cael walked into her room.

"Wh…what are you doing here?"

Shocked, Cael asked, "And why shouldn't I be here?"

"I just thought that maybe...well, this is a lot...to... uh...deal with."

"Sweetheart, that's why I'm here." Bending, he kissed her lips, noting how cold they were. "Are you warm enough? I can get some more blankets."

Still stunned, Regina decided she had no time to try to guess Cael's intentions. "Cael, I thought when you left yesterday, you were saying goodbye."

Planting his hands on his hips, he shook his head. "Regina, what on earth are you talking about? I thought you were sleeping or I would have stayed longer. Of course I said goodbye when I was leaving."

"No, I mean I thought it was *goodbye*...you know, as in forever goodbye."

Blowing out a breath, he sat on the edge of her bed and said, "Okay, maybe we need to establish some basic ground rules."

"Ground rules?" Her eyebrows arched upward as she stared.

"Yes, and the number one rule is, don't assume you know what I'm talking about when you're half asleep."

"But—"

"But, nothing," he asserted, then smiled as he took her hand. "Baby, we just admitted we were in love the other day. Why the hell would I leave now?"

Unable to meet his eyes, she whispered, "Because you've just gone through this with Cindy. Because this won't be pretty...it'll be ugly, and hard, and scary."

"Yes, I did just go through this," he agreed, "and I know how important it is to have people that care about you around. I'll be here for you and my family'll be here for both of us. Yes, it won't be pretty, but you are always beautiful to me. Yes, it'll be hard, but I'll be your soft place to land. And yes, it'll be scary, but that's when we'll cling together and make it through to the other side where there'll be nothing but good."

Tears flowed freely as Cael's words soothed deep inside Regina. His arms wrapped around her, pulling her into his wide chest, enveloping her against his warm body as she sobbed. Finally, she lifted her face and wiped her nose on a tissue from the box.

"Now, baby, let me reiterate…I love you."

Grinning, she said, "I love you, too."

Using his thumbs to wipe the last traces of tears, he said, "Okay…so what's on the agenda for today."

"Let's see…infusion room, chemo, getting freezing cold, starting to throw up…how's that for a full day."

"All right, funny girl." Cael sighed, loving Regina's smile but hating what they were joking about.

"Cael? Can I ask you to do something for me?"

"Anything for you, Red. You know that."

She slid from the bed and went to her small suitcase that Robert had brought to her. Pulling out the clippers, she said, "It's time. I want to get rid of the rest of my hair before it falls out in horrid clumps."

He almost asked if she was sure, but quickly realized that was a stupid question. *She knows what she's doing, so the least I can do, is help her.* "Absolutely." He accompanied her to the bathroom where he stood over her and gently ran the clippers over her short hair, his heart aching at the small reddish cloud that surrounded her as her hair fell to the floor.

When he was finished, she stared into the mirror and ran her hand over her smooth scalp. Sucking in a deep breath, she lifted her gaze and stared at him in the reflection. "Okay," she stated.

He smiled in return, repeating, "Okay."

Hours later, he sat in a chair next to her infusion chair and wrapped the third blanket tighter around her. "Warmer?"

She nodded wanly, her eyes closed as she breathed through her nausea. Later, back in her room, she felt too weak to make it to the bathroom, so she threw up in a pan and he took care of it for her. Finally, she tried to wave him away.

"You didn't sign up for this shit," she groaned.

Kissing the top of her head, he said, "Nothing you do for someone you love is shit."

Glaring at him, while sucking on ice chips, she said, "Where did you hear that?"

He chuckled, "Just made it up, Red." Ducking as she tossed a piece of ice at him, he almost tripped as Miss Ethel walked into the room with Eleanor.

Too exhausted to be embarrassed, Regina mumbled, "Sorry."

Eleanor came up and offered, "I know we didn't get to talk much the other night, but I'm a nurse. Miss Ethel and I would love to sit with you for a while."

She looked at Cael, contrite. "I'm sorry, you haven't even eaten."

"I'm not sorry, but I do need to go talk to someone.

I'll leave you in good hands for a little while." Kissing her cheek, he whispered, "Never forget, I love you."

"Me too," she whispered back and watched as he walked out of the room. Turning her gaze back to the two women in the room, she tried to smooth the covers over her legs, but Miss Ethel jumped in.

"Now lean back and I'm going to put on some soft music while Eleanor helps you with some Jello."

Thinking she would be embarrassed, she quickly found that the two women were efficient and helped tremendously. After a while, she closed her eyes and began to snooze. Vaguely aware they were leaving, she opened her eyes in time to see them exiting just as Cael was walking back into the room. Miss Ethel stopped him with her hand on his arm and he bent down to whisper to her. Miss Ethel smiled and patted his arm before he kissed both women and stepped aside for them to leave.

Barely awake, she whispered, "Hey, Titan."

"Hey, Red," he whispered back, kissing her lips. "I wanted to make it back to say goodnight and let you know I'll see you tomorrow. I've got a meeting in the morning, but I'll see you as soon as I can."

As her eyes closed and sleep took her away, she felt his warm lips on hers once more.

27

"Do you understand the procedure and risks, and still agree?"

"Absolutely," Cael responded before signing the multitude of forms that were placed in front of him.

The doctor in charge of the stem cell donor match program reiterated, "If Ms. Nunzel is not a match for you, this form allows us to use your stem cells for any other patient that would be a match."

"I understand," he replied, and signed again, his leg bouncing in anticipation. "So, we can find out if I'm a match today with a blood test, but regardless, I can start the filgrastim injections?"

"Yes, we can start those today, since you'll be a donor for anyone."

A sound behind them drew his and the doctor's attention to the door, now crowded with men.

"What—" the doctor began.

"We're here to see if we can be donor matches as well," Zander said, as usual taking his place as the eldest.

Cael jumped up from his seat, stalked over, and stared into the faces of his brothers, tears pricking his eyes. "Damn, guys."

"We did a little research and decided that we wanted to donate stem cells as well. If you're not a match for Regina, then maybe one of us is. And, if not, then we'll be helping someone else."

A petite, older administrative assistant pushed her way through the men, at first glaring up at them for interrupting the doctor, then, hearing Zander's offer, her eyes changed from dull to sparkling. "Well, well. Come this way and I'll get you started on the information material."

They all laughed and, with chin lifts to Cael, followed her down the hall. Turning back to the doctor, Cael observed his wide smile.

"It appears you and Ms. Nunzel have got some good friends."

"Yeah…they're my brothers."

Regina lay back in her bed, the side effects of the chemo for the past two weeks having drained her strength, but she could see the end in sight. Cael had been in every day after work, only missing one day when he said he did not feel well. Robbie had finally gotten over his cold and so Robert had been back to visit as well.

She smiled, remembering seeing Cael and Robert talking outside her room one day, their faces intent, but shaking hands afterwards. She wanted the two men in her life to get along and hoped her brother was seeing Cael as someone who was sticking around.

The doctor had been in that morning and announced that they had found a stem cell donor match for her and she should be ready for the transplant within a few days. Grateful, she climbed from the bed and moved into the bathroom. After taking care of business, she showered, glad for the warm water to sooth her tired body. Drying off, she pulled on comfortable sweat pants and thick socks. Eleanor had brought her a long-sleeved, button-up bed jacket in soft pink to keep her warm, while still allowing the IV line easy access.

Staring into the mirror, she smoothed on moisturizer, ignoring her pale complexion and the dark circles. As her gaze drifted up, she rubbed her hand over her bald head, sighing. Feeling cold, she pulled on a soft knit cap and moved back into the room. Eschewing the bed, she sat in the chair, made more comfortable with pillows. Finally wrapping her legs in one of Miss Ethel's knit blankets, she felt ready to face the day.

Settling in with her eReader, she was soon interrupted by a knock on the door. Cael walked in, a smile on his face. Coming over, he bent to kiss her upturned face.

"You look good today, babe."

"I showered and, God, it felt good."

He pulled up a chair and scooted it close to her. "How are you doing? Really, honestly…how are you doing?"

Sucking in her lips, she fought the urge to simply say 'fine'. Blowing out a deep breath, she replied, "Better. The intense chemo is over. The stem cell transplant is in a couple of days. They'll keep me for several more days after that to monitor the side effects. You know…pain, possible infection, more nausea…same old, same old."

Cael's heart hurt, but Regina appeared to be looking forward so he tried to also. "So…the transplant soon."

"Yes. I think they have it scheduled for the day after tomorrow." They settled into a comfortable silence before she asked, "Tell me about your work. I know this is a difficult time to be starting a new job."

Shrugging, he replied, "Benefits of being my own boss—I get to make my own hours. And Terrance gets it. His brother-in-law is a cancer survivor."

Understanding completely what he must have gone through, and to have made it out the other side, she smiled.

"It's actually pretty easy. His uncle's company already had employees and a few contracts they were working on. So, I can go to the site when I can, but my real specialty is the detailed wood work and the sites aren't ready for that yet."

"Where are they?"

"Working in Old Towne right now. A stretch of townhouses needed reconstruction, a lot like your rental."

Regina nodded, thinking of her house, anxious to get back to it and out of the hospital.

Cael watched her for a moment, then, said, "That

brings up something I wanted to talk to you about." She tilted her head but remained silent, so he plunged ahead. "When you get out of here next week…I really don't want you going back to your house all by yourself."

Reaching out to take his hand, she said, "Oh, Cael, I'll be fine. I'll be a little weak—"

"That's what I mean," he stated, his brows lowered. "I'll be at work during the day and afraid for you. Wouldn't it be better to be with someone for a little while?"

Regina thought of his house but the construction was still going on and, with him gone to work, she would still be alone. Biting her lip, she stared at him, waiting for him to continue his thoughts.

"Miss Ethel," he announced.

"I can't impose on her," she protested.

"She wants you to come," he hastened to add. "She's quite insistent." He moved close, his face directly in front of hers. "Please, baby. Let us help you."

She really liked her townhome, but had to admit it was lonely at times. The idea of staying in Miss Ethel's comforting home held appeal. Warm home, comforting food, good company. *Sounds divine.* "Are you sure she doesn't mind?"

A wide smile split his face and he grabbed her cheeks with his hands, kissing her soundly. "She'd be disappointed if you said no," he said, kissing her again.

"Okay," she agreed, relaxing back into her cushions. "I'll do it."

Kissing Regina soundly once more, Cael relished the feel of her lips on his. He missed her body at night, the closeness of holding her tightly. Pulling back, he rubbed her cheeks, seeing the blush heat the skin underneath his thumbs.

"I want you," she confessed, her hands gripping his shoulders. "I miss our walks and talks. I miss the old movies and snuggling after we make love."

"I do too, babe. I promise, when you're well enough, we'll have all that and more." He grinned, and added, "And when I promise something, I never break that promise."

"Oh, God. A Disney quote again. You really are sexy!"

Five days later, the doctor smiled as Cael was giving Regina a goodbye kiss. Winking, Cael called out, "Take care of my girl," as he left the room.

The doctor chatted during his examination, pleased at her progress. "You've responded very well and I anticipate discharging you tomorrow."

"Thank God," she breathed. "I've been dying to get out of here."

"I'll have the nurse come in and give you all the discharge instructions. They are lengthy and very important, so she'll take the time to review them in detail. Make sure to ask any questions you can think of and we'll see you back weekly to monitor your progress."

Nodding enthusiastically, she was willing to agree to anything to be able to leave. Miss Ethel had come by to assure her that she would be thrilled to have her stay with her for a while until she regained her strength.

Several minutes later, a nurse walked into the room, her hands full of papers. "Ready to plan on going home?" she asked, her pretty smile aimed at Regina.

"Yes, please!"

They sat for a while, going over the discharge paperwork carefully. Occasionally asking questions, she made sure she understood everything she needed to do. Finally, with the last of the papers signed and collected, she leaned back, a peaceful sigh sliding from her lips.

"I'm lucky," she said, still smiling. "To get a donor match and have it working so well."

"Well, those handsome male friends of yours were wonderful to all donate. I heard the nurses in the donor office talking about them for days."

Her brow furrowed as she looked at the nurse, but she did not have a chance to ask any questions before the nurse gushed, "And to have your boyfriend be the match? Oh, my. That's so sweet." She stood and gathered the papers, saying, "I'll have copies made and they'll be returned to you when you discharge tomorrow. Good luck, Ms. Nunzel."

Handsome men...donate...boyfriend. Her heart pounded in her chest as her breath caught in her throat. Closing her eyes to the beautiful pain spearing through her, she was unable to keep the huge smile from her face. For a second, she wondered why he kept it a secret, but then remembered her desire to have Cindy's wig be an anonymous donation. *Should I say something?* As the question rolled around in her mind, she knew her answer. *No...it can be his secret gift...and my secret acceptance.*

28

One week later, Regina was ensconced in Miss Ethel's house, currently sitting on the sofa, smiling at the gathering. The room was full and spilled into the entry foyer and dining room, where Miss Ethel and Rosalie had set up trays of sandwiches, and bowls of fruit and chips, and sodas on the table.

Zander sat in one of the cushioned chairs, with Rosalie perched on his lap. Zeke took his usual spot on the floor near Miss Ethel, naturally in her chair, her knitting needles clicking. In the basket on the floor, lay a pile of colorful caps she was knitting for the cancer wings of both the children's hospital and the adult cancer center. Every color, every design, some with knit flowers and others with sports insignias. Regina grinned as she observed the growing pile of caps made by loving hands and touched the one she sported on her head.

Rafe looked up as Eleanor walked into the room, her

hands full of drinks. He jumped up to assist and then settled back on the other end of the sofa with her in his lap.

Asher, quiet as ever but, as she noted, eyes intently taking in everyone in the room, sat in a dining room chair that he moved into the room, his plate balanced on his lap. His gaze landed on hers and a small smile slipped across his lips.

Jayden and Jaxon argued quietly about the game that had been on TV last evening, their conversation often not making sense to anyone else as their twin-language of finishing each other's thoughts and sentences took over. Miss Ethel lifted her eyebrow at them and the two men instantly quieted, causing a giggle to slip out of Regina.

Cael had not arrived yet, having said he needed to pick up something for the impromptu gathering. Hearing a noise from the front hall, she looked that way just as he stuck his head around the corner.

"I brought a visitor today," he announced with a twinkle in his eyes as he gazed at her.

Before she could ask, Cindy popped out from behind him, her face bright with a wide smile and the beautiful hair in her wig glistening in the light of the hall. "Hi, Miss Regina!"

Throwing her arms wide, she watched with glee as the little girl wove between the large men, scrambling to move their feet out of the way. She welcomed her with a huge hug. "Oh, my goodness, it's so nice to see you out of the hospital!" She eyed Kathy and Tom entering the room with Cael and shot them a smile also.

Cindy pulled back and her eyes jumped to Regina's head, her small face scrunched in thought. Feeling the need to show her exactly what she looked like, she pulled off her knit cap, exposing her bald head. Cindy stared for a moment not saying anything and she wondered if she had done the right thing. The room was quiet and just when she started to speak, Cindy said in a small voice, "You gave your hair for my wig."

Smiling, she nodded. "Yes, I did, but it was a simple thing to give, sweetheart."

"But, now you've got no hair."

"Darling, I was going to lose my hair anyway. Giving it to you was a gift worth giving. And, you know what? I don't miss it. I think the most important thing for us to do is focus on being well." She winked, adding, "But, I have to admit…my hair looks good on you."

Cindy giggled for a moment, then stared once more at Regina's head before reaching out to touch the smooth skin. Slowly, she moved her hand back to her own head and slid the wig off. Cindy's hair was starting to grow back, little wisps of hair like a newborn chick, covering her head. "I want to be like you when I grow up," Cindy said, proudly. "I want to be strong and pretty."

"Oh, baby, you already are."

The two of them, one adult woman and one child, stared at each other, their bald heads no longer an issue, as they drew from each other's strength.

There was not a dry eye in the room.

Two months later

Regina slipped from the California-king bed, no longer sitting on the floor, but now on a platform bed frame that included a bookcase headboard. Tiptoeing to the bathroom, the gleaming hardwood floors covered with a dark blue and grey rug gave the master bedroom a homey feel. Once inside, she took care of business before moving to the wide, vanity mirror.

Her complexion was less sallow and a fluff of slightly curly, red-blonde hair covered her head. Now that they were into winter, she still wore a thick cap when she went outside, but inside, she preferred to be natural. Which reminded her, the last time she had been with Cindy, she watched Tangled with her and heard a line she had never paid attention to before.

"You don't really need someone to complete you. You only need someone to accept you completely."

Yeah...natural is the only way to go, cause he accepts me completely.

Stepping into the large, walk-in closet, she donned a pair of yoga pants and threw on a sweatshirt over a tank top. She stood for a moment, staring at her clothes hanging neatly next to his and a smile settled on her lips.

Walking back into the bedroom, she passed a sleeping Cael, the covers down to his waist, giving her a mouth-watering view of his thick muscles and tight abs.

He had worked late finishing the latest site for his company and was looking forward to a weekend with no obligations.

She padded downstairs on her socked feet and headed straight to the coffee maker in the kitchen. Within a few minutes, the scent of strong coffee wafted through the house. Not long after, the sizzle of bacon, cheesy hash browns, and scrambled eggs added to the tantalizing aroma.

Right on time, Cael scuffled into the room, his sweat pants hanging dangerously low on his hips. He accepted to cup of coffee shoved into his hands, but bent to take her lips before his first sip. "Have I told you lately that I love you?"

She giggled, replying, "Um...yes. Last night after we tore up the sheets making love." His chuckle, rough in the early morning, rumbled through her and she sobered, adding, "And I love you too."

"Got something I want to ask you...I know I'm not doing it right, but standing here in our kitchen, seeing all that makes you, *you*, well, I can't wait." He reached into his pocket and pulled out a ring box.

Eyes wide, she gasped, watching as he opened it and pulled out a delicate, white-gold, princess cut diamond ring.

"Heard Cindy ask if she could be a bridesmaid when we got married and you told her yes, when the time was right. It made me realize that I didn't want to wait, Red. The time is now. You and me, forever."

Nodding, she held out her hand and watched as he

slipped the ring on her finger. She stared at it for a moment then clutched his face with her hands, pulling him in for a long kiss. Turning off the stove, she allowed him to pick her up in his arms. Breakfast would have to wait.

Seven Years Later

"We need to hurry," Regina called out.

"Babe, it'll take as long as it takes," Cael replied. His hands were full with four-year-old Jonathan, who insisted on choosing his own clothes and dressing himself. Today, it was the green shorts with a blue Batman shirt, and in his hands he clutched the super-hero cape that had been worn so often it was ratty on the edges.

Finally, scooping him up, he carried him down the stairs where Regina stood with baby Lena in her arms, cute and cuddly in her coordinated pink outfit. Used to her son's eclectic choice of clothing, she grinned as she placed a kiss on his cheek.

"Mom," he complained, looking to his dad for cama-raderie, but Cael's response was to bend, placing a kiss on Regina's lips and then moving to kiss the top of Lena's head.

Picking up Miss Ethel on the way to the park, he assisted her into the back seat, where she insisted on sitting between the two car seats, chatting with Jonathan and cooing at Lena. Once there, she held Jonathan's hand while Regina carried the baby carrier and he carried the picnic basket and blankets. Finding a shady spot near the pond, they spread blankets on the grass and settled down.

He and Jonathan played with a ball while Regina nursed Lena before placing her back in her carrier. Pulling out the picnic items, she placed them on paper plates.

Miss Ethel looked fondly at he and his family, her eyes still as sharp as ever. "My boys were all so good," she said to Regina, pride in her voice.

"Miss Ethel, I think that had everything to do with you," Regina replied, stilling her hands and watching the older woman.

Smiling, Miss Ethel said, "Oh, I think I helped, but I think each one of them had such goodness in them to begin with." She offered a hug to Jonathan as he plopped down on the blanket next to her.

Cael bent to kiss Regina before settling down between her and a sleeping Lena. Soon, the food was eaten and Jonathan was begging his mother to let him feed the ducks. Retrieving the bag of cracked corn she had brought, the two of them wandered to the edge of the pond, tossing out the feed and laughing as the ducks swam quickly to them.

Cael rocked the carrier as Lena stirred slightly and she was soon slumbering again. Looking over at Miss Ethel, he asked, "Are you too hot? We can leave just as soon as you—"

"Oh, hush boy," she laughed. "I'm just fine. In fact, I'm better than fine. I'm with one of my wonderful boys and his beautiful family."

He smiled and nodded as he cast his gaze over Lena and down to the pond where Regina and Jonathan were laughing. "I never thought it could be like this," he said. Seeing her tilted head, he added, "Family. Happy...and *healthy* family. I never thought it would be this way for me."

"Oh, my dear boy," Miss Ethel said, her grey eyes warm on his face as she patted his arm with her frail hand. "Remember what I told you the first night you came to me? Fairytales tell us that evil can be beaten and the happily ever after can come true. You're living proof of that."

Soon, as the sun began to set, the gathering collected their item and walked back toward the parking lot. Miss Ethel held fast to Jonathan's hand and Cael wrapped his arm around Regina, carrying Lena, as the sunset cast them in its glow.

Leaning down, he whispered, "Happy, Red?"

Her wide smile warmed his heart as she replied, "Happily ever after."

Don't miss the next Heroes at Heart
For all of Miss Ethel's boys:
Heroes at Heart (Military Romance)
Zander
Rafe
Cael

Jaxon
Jayden
Asher
Zeke
Cas

Asher

Zeke

Cas

Lighthouse Security Investigations

Mace

Rank

Walker

Drew

Blake

Tate (August 2020)

Hope City (romantic suspense series co-developed

with Kris Michaels

Hope City Duet (Brock / Sean)

Carter

Brody by Kris Michaels

Kyle

Ryker by Kris Michaels

Saints Protection & Investigations

(an elite group, assigned to the cases no one else wants…or
can solve)

Serial Love

Healing Love

Revealing Love

Seeing Love

Honor Love

Sacrifice Love

Protecting Love

Remember Love

Discover Love

Surviving Love

Celebrating Love

Follow the exciting spin-off series:

Alvarez Security (military romantic suspense)

Gabe

Tony

Vinny

Jobe

SEALs

Thin Ice (Sleeper SEAL)

SEAL Together (Silver SEAL)

Letters From Home (military romance)

Class of Love

Freedom of Love

Bond of Love

The Love's Series (detectives)

Love's Taming

Love's Tempting

Love's Trusting

The Fairfield Series (small town detectives)

Emma's Home

Laurie's Time

Carol's Image

Fireworks Over Fairfield

Please take the time to leave a review of this book. Feel free to contact me, especially if you enjoyed my book. I love to hear from readers!

Facebook

Email

Website